We Were Brave

ALSO BY CAP DANIELS

We Were Brave

CAP DANIELS
&
MELISSA MASON

ANCHOR WATCH
PUBLISHING

** USA **

We Were Brave
Cap Daniels & Melissa Mason

Published by:

ANCHOR WATCH
—— PUBLISHING ——
** USA **

13-Digit ISBN: 978-1-951021-50-4
Library of Congress Control Number: 9781951021504

Printed in the United States of America

We Were Brave

CAP DANIELS & MELISSA MASON

FOREWORD
by Dawn Lee McKenna

In June 2017, I was packing for a trip when I got a message from a man named Cap Daniels. He mentioned that he was a huge fan, and he clearly had read my books, and then told me that he was getting ready to release his second book in the *Chase Fulton Series*.

Now, I get a lot of messages and emails similar to that one. They all come right out and tell me what they want from me: they want me to promote them in my newsletter or on my Facebook page. Some of those people have already copied my book covers, my blurbs, or even taken components of my books for their own. I've even had a few people who were actually my "competitors" although there are so many readers that we really don't have to compete. But these few people actually contacted me under false names asking for my help.

All of this is to say that by June of 2017, I'd grown wary of messages like Cap's. Except....

Except, his was so gracious, so humble, so well written. And the only thing he asked me for was a little feedback on his books if I ever had the time or inclination to read one. Because he was so polite, and because he could clearly use words good, I messaged him back and told him that I was packing for a trip and leaving the following day, but that I would read his first book, or at least some of it, when I got back the following week. His answer was just as gracious and self-effacing as his first message, and he was so heartwarmingly grateful. So, I went on about my packing, and set him aside for a week. Except...

Except, an hour later, I grabbed a cup of coffee and his first book, *Opening Chase*. I read three pages and sent him a wall of text. That wall essentially said that he was a fine writer, and that I wanted to help him with the release of his second book the following month.

The long and short of the thing is that I and our mutual friend, Wayne Stinnett, helped him with a launch plan, promoted him to our readers, and then sat back and had the joyful experience of watching him and his lovely wife get completely blindsided. You see, he didn't ask for our help. But even if he had, he would have had no idea what to expect. He hoped to sell one-hundred books that day. He sold far more than that in the first hour. And now, he's a bestselling thriller author, with seven Chase books under his belt, and he doesn't need my help anymore. Except...

Except, after Hurricane Michael decimated both his sailboat and the towns where my books are set, he wrote a novella called *I Am Gypsy*. He wrote it and donated the profits to the victims of Hurricane Michael. Victims like himself, but I think he forgot that.

He wrote the book from the perspective of a sailboat, and that sailboat was his own, mortally-wounded *Gitana*, which means gypsy.

I'm not sure if many readers would understand—or even stop to wonder—what kind of gift it takes to make a sailboat live, breathe, speak, love and weep. Cap is fond of saying that I'm a literary genius yackity smackity of our generation blah blah, but I couldn't do what he did. I wept through the entire thing, and texted him throughout. I cried, but the novella was a joyous thing. It was balletic and beautiful, wrenching and inspiring, tragic and yet hopeful. I also told him, quite genuinely, that his little novella that he wrote in a week or so had just become one of my five favorite books of all time. Right up there with *Cold Mountain*.

In one of the many messages I sent him as I read, I told him the most important thing I've ever said to him, besides "I love you." I told him that he was a fine thriller writer, but his gift was for something altogether different. It was for books like *Gypsy*.

There's nothing wrong with writing thrillers, and there's honor in giving his readers the respect of writing them well. But in *I Am Gypsy*, and now, in *We Were Brave*, all of Cap's heart, character, humility and integrity are just laid out there on the page, and in words that are so deftly and skillfully written.

I was honored when the man who has become my dear friend—even an adopted brother—asked me to read the first chapter of *We Were Brave*. I cried again; not because anything tragic or sad happened in those first scenes, but because I read the words and heard *Gypsy* speaking. Cap was actually writing what he has always been meant to write.

Moreover, Melissa Mason's grace, dignity, and beauty shine through the words in this book. The only way to improve on Cap's gift, is to add Melissa's gift to it. I believe they're about to become the Tracy and Hepburn of contemporary fiction.

You're in for a wonderful experience with this book, and with all of his books that are yet to be written.

Dawn Lee McKenna

PART I

CHAPTER 1
The Coffee Shop

I was in that ratty coffee shop in the corner of that ratty bookstore for only one reason: it was warm. In the interest of honesty, there was one more reason: Linda, the barista, snuck me coffee when the manager wasn't looking. It was February 29, 2012, and I didn't know it at the time, but it would soon be the day everything about my life changed forever.

I loved bookstore coffee shops, but not for their climate control or charity coffee. I used to move my books to the front table, alongside, and occasionally on top of the latest releases by James Patterson and Stephen King. Then I camped out in a bean bag chair near the windows and clocked how long it took for some unsuspecting customer to pick up my book and read the jacket. It usually took less than ten minutes, and then usually less than ten minutes after that, the reader would walk out the door with one of my books and a free bookmark inside a heavy paper bag with fibrous handles. Another dollar and eighty-five cents was deposited in my royalty account. That was a long time ago, before my past caught up with my present and dropped a big steaming pile right on top of my future.

My name is Cap Millhouse. Or at least it used to be. I guess our names have almost nothing to do with our identity. They're merely labels, like the Dewey Decimal System number taped to the spine of every book in every library all over the world. We all have a name, and its only purpose is to make us easier to find. For me, my name had no meaning since I didn't want to be found anymore. There was a day, too long ago to remember, when someone would stare at me with that "Aren't you Cap Millhouse?" look. It had been flattering once. I'd signed a few books and a couple of publishing contracts I believed at the time were my ticket to ride, but some rides are taken on roads a bit rockier than others. And my road has been one of the rockiest.

Writing was the recommendation of a second-rate psychiatrist at the VA hospital whose name I can't recall.

"Writing can be incredibly cathartic, Captain Millhouse. Have you ever considered jotting down the things that bother you? A journal, or a diary, or simply a notebook? It doesn't matter what you call it."

That was the last thing on Earth I wanted to do. I didn't want to talk about it, write about it, think about it, or even remember it. I wanted it to go away. That's what my two best friends at the time encouraged me to do: forget about it, one bottle at a time. My friends, the only ones I thought I'd have for what remained of my life, were Jim and Jack...Beam and Daniels.

What put me on that couch in front of that government shrink was something no twenty-six-year-old Army captain should ever have to endure.

"Tell me about the accident," the doctor said.

The only thing that angered me more than him asking questions in the form of statements was his expectation for me to respond. "Tell me your first name," I said.

"It would be best if you called me Doctor—"

"It would be best if I never had to come back to this hospital and lie on this couch and answer questions that aren't really questions. Why the hell can't you just *ask* a question?"

He scribbled on his yellow legal pad, occasionally glancing over the top of his half-glasses perched on the tip of his hawksbill nose. If his nose were as wide as it were long, it would render the man blind.

Maybe I was wrong about the order of things that made me mad. Maybe him writing on the legal pad I never got to see was what made me angrier than anything else.

What is he writing? I thought. *What did I say that's worthy of being written down? Is it what I said or how I said it? Is it both?*

"You read the file, d-o-c-t-o-r. It was no accident. It was a fu—" I was still sane enough back then to know when I was pushing too hard or when I'd been pushed too hard. It wasn't always easy, but most of the time, I could still control my temper. I took a few deep breaths and watched that S.O.B. write on his top-secret yellow legal pad. "It wasn't an accident, doc. It was an ambush, and I know you've read the file."

He pocketed his pen, shoved his half-glasses atop his head, and interlaced his fingers across his chest. "Yes, I've read the file, Captain, but the file doesn't tell me how you felt during the encounter. It only tells me the facts as you recalled them at the time. We can't change the facts, but we might be able to change the effects your perceptions of those facts have on you."

Was that a question? And has he upgraded the accident to an encounter?

I can't remember how long I stared at him, but I know it became comically long. Or perhaps my laughter was simply my mind's way of changing the subject.

"So, Captain Millhouse, tell me about the...ambush."

From accident to encounter to ambush. Maybe we're making some progress.

He obviously wasn't going to let me change the subject with laughter or any other mechanism. The one thing I knew for certain back then was that talking about it wasn't going to change anything, especially how it made me feel, no matter what the government shrink called it.

"If I write about it, do I still have to tell you about it?"

The half-glasses came down from his shiny bald head and landed precisely where they'd been on that god-awful nose. The pen reemerged from his shirt pocket, and once again, the yellow legal pad became the doctor's focus. When he finished his scribbling, another of those damned non-questions came falling out of his mouth. "Good. So you're going to write about it."

Again came the pause as he awaited my response or reaction, which aren't the same things, and I was sure that even a government shrink knew the difference. Perhaps he was writing down my reactions and ignoring my responses, or vice versa.

Breathing through my nose in a conscious effort to avoid ripping off one of his discount rack loafers and beating him to death with it, I hissed, "I didn't say I was going to write about it."

He stuck the butt of the pen into the corner of his mouth and watched my hands. Suddenly, I was self-conscious of my fingers. My nails, what was left of them, were chewed well into the quick, and my thumbs were still twisted inhumanly outward, looking far more like deformed eagle talons than appendages belonging to a human hand. The thumbs, if they could still be considered such, were the most obvious physical evidence of what the shrink called "the encounter."

I tried to hide my hands, but doing so only made my self-consciousness more obvious, and I suspected the legal pad was about to receive another application of ink.

"Why do I have to do either?"

"Either of what?" he asked.

He just asked a real question in the form of a question. Alex Trebek would be so proud.

"Why do I have to write about it or talk about it?"

"I'm not ordering you to do either. I'm just doing my job."

"Your job," I scoffed. "Is that what you call it? Is that what you get paid to do? Force the people you're supposed to be helping to do things they don't want to do?"

He clicked his pen closed. "I can't force anyone to do anything. Feeling forced makes people feel powerless. Surely, you don't believe I want you to feel powerless."

"For God's sake, doc. Just ask a question. Look me in the eye and ask me a question. Can you do that? Just once? Can you?"

The glasses came off. "Captain Millhouse, do you feel guilty because you survived?"

CHAPTER 2
Everything is a Weapon

When the spiral begins, one of the first extravagances to disappear is grooming, and there was a time when I was aggressively defensive when anyone stared at me. Back when I taught English at the University of Tennessee, it was fashionable for professors to let their hair grow and even sport a beard, but my days of looking like DJ Johnny Fever from *WKRP in Cincinnati* had given way to unkempt, unclean, and quickly graying. By the time I'd accepted the fact that my life had devolved into hiding in a bookstore trying to stay warm and drinking charity coffee, I no longer cared if curious, disgusted eyes lingered on what was left of me. At that point, I was nothing more than a grotesque shell of the man I could have been.

The February darkness comes early in the foothills of the Great Smoky Mountains, and with it comes the plummeting temperatures that spell misery punctuated by death for people with nowhere to sleep. I'd spent too many nights at the bus station and inside the dumpster behind the paper company. Though enough paper can be adequate insulation to keep the body alive through the fourteen-hour nights, it won't keep a man warm. I considered myself lucky. I'd found a shelter that would let me sleep on a cot under a real blanket, but the doors were locked until around nine o'clock every night. The coffee shop and bookstore closed at eight.

I pawned my watch years before and discovered I never really needed it after all. If knowing the precise time was ever necessary, and I found it rarely was, there was always a clock somewhere or someone who had a watch. Existence on the street isn't measured in hours and minutes. It's measured in sunsets and sunrises. If I could make it through the long winter night, even inside a dumpster, the daylight was always easier than the darkness.

In return for letting me sleep on a worn-out army cot, the shelter required that I listen to a preacher tell me how much God loved me and about the Heaven awaiting the faithful. Somewhere, an all-powerful, loving, benevolent God reigned on high, and I was hiding out in a bookstore coffee shop and wearing the same clothes I'd worn for weeks.

I didn't look forward to the hour I'd spend outside between the closing of the bookstore and, hopefully, the opening of the shelter doors. Sometimes they couldn't find volunteers to work the shelter, so other walking corpses like me would huddle together in the alley, praying for anything flammable that might keep the frostbite at bay until the doors opened. The bank sign across the street showed eighteen degrees at 7:41 p.m. It was sixteen the night before, so there was a tiny glimmer of hope.

The northern hemisphere was once again slowly tilting southward since the winter solstice had passed. The days were getting longer, and with every degree of descent, I was moving ever so slightly closer to the sun.

"I'm going to throw these out if you don't want them." Linda's voice was husky and coarse from too many years of smoking, but her kindness was more than I deserved.

I let my weary eyes meet hers. "Thank you, Linda."

I took the three muffins and crammed two of them into my coat pockets. I'd found an old Army field jacket on the loading dock behind the Salvation Army donation center and decided it was almost big enough to fit me. There was no liner, so it was little more than a heavy overshirt, but it was a layer, and it had nice big pockets perfect for day-old muffins.

Okay, I didn't really *find* the field jacket. I'd stolen it. One of the men who'd been unloading a truck took it off and tossed it onto the loading dock. He must've forgotten about it when he went inside, and I took that as a sign he'd abandoned the jacket. To a homeless guy whose only means of support are charity and theft, the line separating the two is practically nonexistent. It was easy for me to believe he'd intentionally left the coat lying on the dock just for me.

Linda was wiping down the counters, emptying coffee pots, and doing all the things necessary to close the coffee bar and pastry shop. As if she had a checklist, she did the same things in the same order every night. Routine is comforting. Chaos is maddening.

Chaos wasn't the only maddening element of my life. The absence of hope for a better tomorrow left me wondering why I cared if I woke up the next morning. I had no family, at least none who would admit I was even a leaf on the family tree. I had no prospect of life inside the realm of normalcy. I was relegated to the alleyways, bus stations, and run-down coffee shops inside forgotten bookstores, and to that place in the far reaches of most people's minds where vermin and pestilence reside. No one would mourn my passing. No one would notice if I didn't show up at the shelter or the coffee shop or the dumpster behind the paper company. I was a forgotten soul, lost in the midst of things society is too busy to acknowledge.

I pulled on my stolen field jacket, preparing for the frigid, hour-long expedition between the bookstore and shelter. Instantly, I realized the next few minutes of my life would either end my suffering or leave me even more entrenched in the underbelly of darkness that had been my home for over a decade.

The slide of a pump shotgun is impossible to mistake for anything else. It's like the buzz of a zipper or the rustling of a bag of potato chips. When such noises happen, a visceral reaction occurs in the brain. Hearing a zipper elicits the need to go to the bathroom. The crunch of a bag sends the sensation of salty decadence onto our tongues. The sound of a shotgun touches another portion of the brain: the part that ignites the fight-or-flight response.

Fight and flight are not the only two solutions that happen in the brain when a threat is detected. The third is also an F-word and often the deadliest of the three: freeze. That's the deer-in-the-headlights reaction and the most common response to a perceived threat. Statistically, almost no one fights. They either flee or freeze.

I heard two shotgun slides cycling almost simultaneously, resurrecting some long-forgotten instinct. My vision became crystal clear, and absolute awareness of everything in my environment overtook me.

"Put your right hand on top of your head, and do it now. Now!" The first gunman's voice echoed through the cavernous space like rolling thunder across a prairie.

It wasn't a conscious decision on my part, but I allowed my body to slide from the chair in which I'd been sitting for hours and slink behind the janitorial closet door Linda had left ajar.

"Using only your left hand, open the cash register and place the money in the bag."

Each of the two gunmen laid a nondescript paper bag on the counter. Gunman number one was at the bookstore cash register, and gunman number two was inches behind Linda at the coffee shop counter.

I watched in silent appraisal of the thieves and made a mental inventory of the closet where I'd taken temporary refuge: seven empty glass coffee pots, three mops, two brooms, one mop bucket, cases of paper cups, lids, napkins, jugs of cleaning products, and four fluorescent tube bulbs. Everything is a weapon when the environment—and its occupants—are hostile enough.

It was twenty-five feet to gunman number two and seventy-five feet to gunman one—targets of opportunity. I had no way to engage the first gunman across the store, but number two was well within my range.

I was the only customer, and Linda and the girl at the register were the only two employees in sight. The assistant manager was in the back office while her two employees were having a night they'd never forget... if they survived.

The gunmen weren't amateurs. They handled their shotguns not like clumsy thugs, but as though the weapons were extensions of their own bodies. The two men were practiced, well-trained, and confident. Unlike nervous first-time criminals, they wasted no time in their efforts to collect exactly what they came to take.

The girl at the register followed the instructions of the first gunman to the letter, opening the register and placing the money into his bag.

Five feet nine inches tall, one hundred ninety pounds. Six feet tall, two hundred ten pounds. Both men are manageable hand to hand, but what am I going to do about those shotguns?

Linda neither fled nor fought. She froze.

Come on, Linda. Don't make him shoot you. Just give him the money.

There couldn't have been more than a few hundred dollars in both registers combined. It hardly seemed like a viable armed-robbery target, but regardless of its viability, the bookstore and coffee shop were shoulder-deep in a fully survivable hostile situation if both women could keep their cool and do as they were told.

I don't think either gunman saw me, and that gave me a sliver of an advantage, but I had no gun, no knife, and even worse, no plan.

As Linda stood motionless and unblinking behind a waist-high countertop, gunman number two grew more and more agitated. "Open the register, and put the money in the bag. Don't make me shoot you."

He drove the barrel of his shotgun into Linda's chest, and she trembled. It was all too much for her to handle. She was in sensory overload, and she wasn't coming back.

The gunman's left foot began to twitch—a definite sign he was within seconds of pulling the trigger. Linda still wasn't moving, and her frozen posture had the potential to spell death for the woman who'd been more kind to me than I could ever deserve.

I grabbed one of the long fluorescent tube lights and hurled it toward the front window of the store, where it exploded instantly upon contact. Both gunmen flinched and spun toward the crash. I sprang from the closet and began closing the distance toward gunman number two. The seven strides it took to eat up the empty space between us seemed to take hours, and the whole event played out in slow motion.

I hurled a glass coffee pot through the air and watched it hit its mark, the side of the gunman's head. The muzzle of the shotgun struck the countertop as the gunman shook off the blow from the glass pot. Everything I'd been taught a quarter-century before about how to fight came pouring back as the man raised the deadly weapon to bear on me. With swiftness I'd forgotten I possessed, I yanked the weapon from the gunman and sent him to the ground with a solid strike to his head.

As he fell, I yelled at Linda, "Get down and call the cops!"

I pulled the shotgun to my shoulder and crouched behind a massive wooden garbage bin. Glancing up to make sure Linda had followed my instructions, I heard the roar of the first gunman's weapon and watched my friend melt to the floor behind the counter.

My life had no value before the sun went down, and at that moment, it had even less. Instead of saving Linda's life, I'd taken it from her with my foolish attempt to play the hero. My heart pounded inside my chest as I abandoned my training and instinct for self-preservation.

Screaming at the top of my lungs, I leapt from behind the bin and charged the first gunman, determined to end his life and save the cashier's. He'd get off at least one shot, and there was nothing I could do to prevent that. My consolation was his shot would be aimed at me and not at the innocent, terrified woman behind the register.

Like an enraged bull, I thundered toward the man, pulling the trigger and racking the pump with every other stride. I watched his finger turn white as he squeezed the trigger, but I didn't flinch. I continued closing the distance and firing as quickly as the weapon would cycle.

The shot was coming, but I didn't care. I got off at least three shots before his gun roared, belching orange flames from the muzzle. The impact felt like being hit by a thousand city buses, but I didn't immediately go down. The world in front of me turned first crimson and then slowly gray.

The cashier was screaming, but I heard no sound escaping her mouth. I couldn't hear anything except the ringing in my ears as I fell face-first to the cold, hard floor.

CHAPTER 3
Help Me

VA Hospital, Johnson City, TN
1993
(Nineteen years earlier.)

"You wanted me to write it down. You said it'd be cathartic. Isn't that the word you used? Cathartic?"

I threw the spiral-bound book onto the doctor's lap, and he ignored it and set his eyes on mine.

"And I suspect, even though you won't admit it, the exercise was cathartic."

There it was, his first nonquestion of the session.

"Can we please have one day when you ask actual questions? Huh, doc? Do you think that might be possible?"

Out came the yellow legal pad, and my anxiety welled up.

As if he sensed my angst rising, he laid the pad facedown on the arm of his chair. "Okay, Captain Millhouse. Here's my first question for the day." He held up my composition book. "Do you want me to read this?"

"You're the one who told me to write it. Why wouldn't you read it?"

He stared at the book and then back at me. "I didn't tell you to write it. I asked if you'd ever thought about writing it down."

I shook my head. "There you go again, playing word games. I thought you were supposed to help me get over what happened down there. I thought that was your job. I think you're playing with me to see how far you can push me before I crack and do something crazy. Then you can arrest me and put me away so you don't have to deal with someone like me."

He tilted his head. "Is that what you think, Captain Millhouse? That the VA wants to lock you up? Have you done anything to warrant being locked up?"

"Look, read it or don't. I don't care. But I wrote it down because you told me it would be cathartic. Well, it wasn't. It was a colossal waste of time that made me wish I'd never come back."

He stuck the stem of his glasses into the corner of his mouth. "It made you wish you'd never come back where? To see me?"

"No." I pushed the corner of the rug into a triangular pile. "I wish I'd never come back from Colombia."

I didn't expect him to smile, but he did. It may have been a self-satisfied smile, but maybe it was another one of his games to push my buttons.

"Tell me about the accident, Captain."

I gritted my teeth. "It wasn't an accident. It was an ambush. Do you know the difference between an accident and an ambush?"

"Perhaps I don't," he said. "Why don't you tell me the difference?"

I stood and paced to the window, wanting nothing more than to dive through the glass and never see him or that room again. "An accident, doctor, is when you spill your drink at a dinner party. An ambush is when the enemy knows where you're going to be and when you're going to be there. An ambush is when a superior force lies in wait and then starts pumping RPGs into the sky like bottle rockets over a damned river full of piranhas and crocodiles. Did you get that, doc? Did you?" He didn't speak, and I didn't turn around. "I guess you didn't, so let me say it again. An ambush is when the enemy knows where you're going to be and when you're going to be there. How the hell could they have known that information? Can you tell me that?"

When I turned around, he was scribbling on the pad, and I'd reached my limit. I stormed across the room, yanked it from his grasp, and shredded it into more pieces than I could count. The doctor never flinched. Instead, he sat stoically, watching me throw a tantrum like a spoiled child.

My breath was coming hard, and I could feel my face flushing bright red. "There! Now help me, Doctor Murphey."

That was his name: Murphey. I knew I'd remember.

"What do you want me to do for you?"

I melted back onto the couch, covered in sweat and panting as if I'd sprinted a mile. "I want you to help me. I want to sleep again. I want to forget about what happened down there, and I want to be normal."

"Normal doesn't exist, John. From soccer moms to the president, everyone has something in their past that comes back to haunt them in quiet, lonely places. It's all part of having been on the planet for more than twenty-five years."

"No, it isn't. Soccer moms never had a helicopter shot out from under them in the jungle with six damned good men in the back. The president never felt the tail rotor separate from his chopper in the middle of the night, ten feet above the jungle canopy. And you.... How about you, doc? Have you ever had a Colombian drug cartel drag you by your feet facedown through the jungle?"

He ran his tongue over his top teeth. "No, Captain, I've never experienced that, and I'm not going to tell you what I've been through is in any way comparable to what you endured, but I will help you."

I suddenly felt like a scared child. "You will?"

"Yes, I will. We've made enormous strides here today. I'm going to start you on some medication—"

"No! I'm not taking any pills. I'm not giving up like that."

Dr. Murphey stood and began untucking his shirt.

"What are you doing, doc?"

He continued untucking his shirt until he'd pulled it well above his stomach, revealing an eight-inch scar across his abdomen. "Do you know what this is?"

I shook my head.

"I took two rounds in my gut during the conflict in the Falkland Islands in 1982. One of those rounds landed in my pancreas. Do you know what the pancreas does?"

"I don't know," I admitted.

"It has two primary purposes: an endocrine function that produces insulin, and an exocrine function that produces digestive enzymes. The portion of my pancreas that produces insulin is fine, but the other portion will never function again."

He pulled a yellow bottle of pills from his pocket and shook it in front of me. "I take these pills before every meal I eat, and I will for the rest of my life. If I didn't, my body wouldn't digest the food I eat, and I'd be dead in a matter of days. Am I giving up by taking these pills?"

I shook my head in short, jerky motions. "No, but it's not the same. You were injured and—"

He put his hand on my knee. "That's right. *We* were injured. Mine was physical, and yours is psychological. In many ways, yours is far more deadly. The medication will help stabilize the chemicals produced by your brain, exactly like these pills provide the enzymes my body requires to digest food."

I wanted to put up a fight, but I was running out of ammunition. "Would I have to take the drugs forever?"

He tucked his shirt back into his trousers and reclaimed his seat. "That's impossible to answer at this point. Treating the mind is not as simple as treating the body. It's far more complex, and in many ways, it's more an art than a science. We'll start you on a simple cocktail of two different drugs. One will help stabilize your mood, and the other will help you sleep. Sleep is the closest thing there is to magic. Once we get that regulated, you'll be amazed how much better you'll feel. Are you willing to give the drugs a chance?"

* * *

University of Tennessee Medical Center, Knoxville, TN
March 1, 2012

"Sir, can you tell me your name?"

I blinked as I came awake, and the outline of a woman's head and shoulders loomed above in the fluorescent glow of the bright white lights.

"Sir, tell me your name."

I licked my lips, and they felt like sandpaper. When I opened my mouth to speak, the words came out in raspy, hoarse croaks. "Where am I?"

"You're at UT Hospital. You were involved in a shooting last night, but you're going to be all right. Can you tell me your name?"

"A shooting? What are you talking about?"

"We need to know your name, sir."

Images were sharpening as my focus returned. "Why do you need to know my name?"

"So we can contact your family and let them know you're all right."

"Can I have something to drink?"

"Sure, you can. I'll get you some water."

I continued blinking. "No, like a whiskey. Whatever you have is fine."

"I'm sorry, sir, but water will have to do. I am going to need your name, though."

"If I tell you my name, can I have a whiskey?"

"No, sir. All you can have is water. How do you feel?"

"Thirsty."

The woman delivered the water in a paper cup about the size of a shot glass, and for just a moment I thought she'd come through with that whiskey. I was wrong, but the water felt good on my throat.

"Thank you."

"You're welcome," she said. "Now, how about your name?"

"Cap, Cap Millhouse. And I don't have any family. No one cares if I'm okay or not."

"Well, Mr. Millhouse, I'm sure that isn't true. There must be somebody."

I slowly shook my head as the events of the previous night began to play inside my memory. "Where's my field jacket? I had two muffins in the pockets. I'm going to need those muffins."

The woman, who I'd determined to be a nurse, looked down at me with a sympathetic, almost motherly smile. "We'll make sure you have plenty to eat, but right now, I need you to rest. The doctor will be in to talk to you in a few minutes."

"Dr. Murphey?"

She furrowed her brow. "No. Dr. Blankenship, the surgeon. He'll be in shortly. Is Dr. Murphey your primary care physician?"

I squinted, trying to make sense of what was happening. "No. Dr. Murphey is a shrink at the VA. I'm a...I mean I *was* a patient there."

"Are you taking any prescription medication, Mr. Millhouse?"

The timeline of my life felt scrambled and twisted in my head. "I don't know."

The nurse looked confused. "You don't know if you're taking any medication?"

I licked my lips again. "Could I have some more water?"

She poured from a Styrofoam pitcher and offered the small paper cup again.

"Thank you."

I swallowed the cold water and relished the feeling of it gliding down my throat. "My muffins...."

"You're not going to be needing your muffins. We'll make sure you have plenty to eat."

"But Linda gave me those muffins. I need them."

"Is Linda your wife?"

I felt bitterness on my tongue as my mind replayed the scene of Linda crumpling to the ground in the coffee shop."

"No, she was just someone who was kind to me. I think I got her killed last night."

The nurse looked down at me as if she had no idea what I was talking about.

"She was the woman," I said. "The woman from the coffee shop last night."

"Mr. Millhouse, Linda isn't dead."

CHAPTER 4
Did You Hurt Anyone?

VA Hospital, Johnson City, TN
1993

"If this is what your drugs are supposed to do to me, I don't want them."

Dr. Murphey pulled off his glasses and pursed his lips. "Tell me what you think the drugs are doing to you."

"It's not what I *think* they're doing. It's what they *are* doing. I feel like a zombie. Oh, I'm sleeping like a hibernating bear, but I want to sleep all the time. I can't study. I can't watch TV. I can't do anything. I'm falling asleep in class."

"Class?" he asked.

"Yeah, class. I'm back in school. I told you that."

"Perhaps you did, but you also tore up my notes in a fit of rage, so remind me."

"It wasn't rage. It was...well, something less than rage. I was just upset."

"It's okay to be upset, John. We'll work on how you react to things that upset you. Now, tell me about school."

"What do you want to know?"

"What are you studying? Where are you going? How are your grades?"

"Doc, I think we're making some real progress. You just asked three real questions in a row."

He ignored my sarcasm, awaiting my answers.

"Okay, I'm working on my master's degree in English at UT, and my grades are good enough to stay in the post-grad program."

"English? Really?"

"Yeah, really. What, you don't think I'm smart enough to study English?"

He tilted his head. "No, that's not at all what I think. I believe you are remarkably intelligent. I'm just surprised you chose English. What's your undergraduate degree?"

"Brace yourself. It was English."

"And the Army chose to make you a pilot?"

"Military intelligence, doc. What can I say? There's not much need for English teachers in the Army. They don't care if you know the difference between an adverb and a pronoun as long as you can kill people and break things."

"So, that's what you believe? That the Army only wants people who kill and break things?"

I gave his question the two seconds of thought it deserved. "Well, yeah, pretty much. There's always going to be cooks and clerks, but for the most part, they want you to be able to pull a trigger when a trigger needs to be pulled. I showed some aptitude for flight, so they sent me to flight school. You were an officer, right?"

He studied the tips of his loafers. "No, actually, I was enlisted, but this isn't about me."

"Sure, it is. We can talk about you, too. Can't we?"

He almost smiled. "We're not supposed to."

"I wasn't supposed to get shot down by a bunch of cocaine dealers with rocket-propelled grenades either, but it happened. What was your MOS?"

"My military occupational specialty isn't important. What is important is that you're here to get better, and I'm here to make sure that happens."

"Come on, doc. I won't tell. What did you do in the Army?"

"Talking with patients about my personal life is not something I'm comfortable doing, Captain."

"Oh, so now we're back to Captain instead of John. I thought we'd moved past that, but okay, I get it. All my personal stuff—the stuff that keeps me up at night and makes me crazy—that's what we're allowed to talk about, but yours is off-limits. I get it."

"That's not how it is, Cap...John."

"Sure it is, and that's okay. I understand." For the first time, he sat in his wingback chair without a pen in his hand and a notepad on his lap. "So, back to the medication. You said it makes you drowsy throughout the day."

"That's right. I don't have any energy, and all I want to do is sleep. Is that what it's supposed to do to me? Because if that's it, I'm out. I can't deal with that."

He shook his head. "No, that's not how the medicine should work. I told you we would have to modify your medication and dosages over time. I'm going to prescribe a change in dosage, but we're going to keep you on the same medication. Are you okay with that?"

"The truth is, I'm not okay with being on drugs at all, but I have to tell you...I'm not reliving what happened down there every night. Whatever's in those drugs, it's working. I just can't spend the rest of my life walking around like a zombie."

He nodded. "That's actually encouraging. And you're right. You shouldn't be sleepy all the time. The new dosages will help."

He was right. The new dosages were much better. I slept regularly, I could study, stay awake in class, and almost live a normal life. There were still moments when I wanted to drive a stake into my eye, but ninety percent of the time, I was almost normal. It was that ten percent of my life that qualified as my own private Hell on Earth.

Perhaps my math isn't graduate quality. Ten percent of my day would be two point four hours, and that isn't the amount of time I spent wanting to drive spikes in my eyes. It was more like twenty minutes every day. The rational part of my brain tried to convince me that I could endure anything for twenty minutes, but what happened inside my head during those twelve hundred seconds every day made me feel like I was drowning while on fire. It wasn't the memory of what I endured in the jungle that tortured me during those twenty minutes. And it wasn't the mistakes I made that cost the lives of the men for whom I was responsible. It was the unthinkable act I perpetrated when I returned from the Central American wilderness that tormented me, and nothing, not even Dr. Murphey's drugs, could grant me a reprieve from the agonizing guilt crushing my soul.

* * *

VA Hospital, Johnson City, TN
1994

"It's good to see you, John. How are you?"

That was a good sign. Dr. Murphey opened the session with a real question.

"I'm doing okay, doc. The meds seem to be doing what they're designed to do. School is going well. I'm even planning to stay for my Ph.D."

"That's fantastic," he said, with what appeared to be real sincerity.

"I think so, too."

He made a brief note on the legal pad, and I didn't mind. Honestly, I didn't care what the note said. I declared that to be a victory.

"So, what do you plan to do with a Ph.D in English? I assume you plan to continue studying English."

"I want to write." My answer surprised me. I hadn't realized writing was my goal. I hadn't let myself declare a goal beyond earning my doctorate.

Dr. Murphey tossed the legal pad aside. "Oh, really? What do you want to write?" Apparently, I wasn't the only one in the room surprised by my answer.

I instantly felt like the dog who'd just caught the delivery truck. I had no idea what to do or say next.

Dr. Murphey showed some mercy. "This is the first time you've said it out loud, isn't it?"

I let a sheepish grin grow on my face. "I guess it is. I wasn't ready to answer any questions about it. I'm sorry."

"No, no, no. Don't apologize. That's what this office is for: revelations and realizations. When you came to me for the first time last year, you couldn't string two sentences together without lashing out at me, my legal pad, or the world in general. Now you're going for your doctorate and planning to write the next great American novel. Novels...right?"

"Yeah, doc. I think so. I think I'll write novels."

He smiled. "I think you should. Now let's talk about life outside of school. How are you sleeping?"

I knew we'd get to that part, but I wasn't looking forward to it. For me, school and books were my life.

"I'm sleeping okay. Six or seven hours a night. I'm eating right, exercising some, but not enough. And check this out." I held up my thumbs, wiggling them like worms. "My thumbs are healing. I've even got some feeling in the left one."

He watched my thumbs for several seconds and then let his smile become a thin horizontal line. "How about the memories?"

I stared at my shoes, wishing I could crawl under the rug. I shrugged and expected him to ask what the shrug meant, but he tilted his head and stared at me. That must be a shrink tactic. Cops use it, too.

"I still struggle sometimes, but it's probably not what you think."

He stared without changing expressions. I felt like I needed to take a breath so deep I could talk for an hour without breathing again. I wanted to tell him about my guilt, but I couldn't tell him what I'd done, no matter how long he stared at me.

"I still think a lot about what happened down there and the men I couldn't save, but that's not the worst of it." The self-loathing welled up inside of me, and my eyes glistened with the tears I would not cry.

Dr. Murphey leaned forward, placed his elbows on his knees, and looked into my eyes. "Whatever it is, John, we can work through it. The medication can't erase the memories. That's not what it's for. It simply gives us the tools we need to deal with our past and present. It sounds like your present is pretty terrific."

I nodded and swallowed hard. "Yeah, it is. It's good right now. I'm good right now. Most of the time. It's just...I mean...I did something wrong. Absolutely wrong. And I can't undo it. I can't un-ring that bell."

The lines on the doctor's forehead slowly formed a long, swooping V, like the wings of a gull against the sky. It was a look of concern punctuated with possible fear. I couldn't let my eyes meet his. Perhaps it was embarrassment or shame, but maybe they're the same thing wearing different nametags.

"John, did you hurt someone?"

I slowly nodded my head as I let my eyelids close.

"John, if you've hurt someone, I have an obligation to report that to the authorities."

My lips formed the words before I realized they'd escaped my tongue. "It's not that kind of hurt. There's no authority for what I did. There's no one to whom it should be reported, and it's not against the law—at least not the criminal code. But that doesn't make what I did okay."

He leaned back in his chair and watched me for what must have been an eternity. "Whatever it is, as long as you haven't physically harmed yourself or anyone else, we can work through it."

"No, you don't work through what I did. It never goes away. And I'm pretty sure there are no tools to deal with it in your pill bottles or anywhere else."

CHAPTER 5
Not So Good Samaritan

University of Tennessee Medical Center
March 1, 2012

"What do you mean Linda's not dead? I was there. I saw what happened."

Clearly unfazed, the nurse smiled beautifully. "Miracles happen every day, Mr. Millhouse. Trust me. I see them. Your friend Linda was very lucky, and the Lord was obviously on her side. I'm not really allowed to talk about other patients, but from what I hear, I think you deserve to know."

"Know what?"

"Linda did get shot, but the bullet hit her hand. She's going to be fine."

"No, that's not right. I saw her go down. And it wasn't a bullet; it was buckshot."

The nurse kept grinning and shrugged. "I don't know what to tell you, Mr. Millhouse, but I know for a fact that Linda, the woman from the bookstore coffee shop, is recovering from hand surgery, and she's going to be fine. I'll even bring her in to see you if you want, but that'll have to wait 'til we get you up to your room."

"I'm sure you're mistaken."

She shrugged again. "Oh, here comes the doctor. I'll be back to check on you in a bit, okay?"

I watched her scurry away as a tall, lean man in scrubs shuffled in. "Hello, I'm Dr. Blankenship. You're looking good for a man who was shot in the chest a few hours ago." He wasted no time going to work. With a tiny penlight he pulled from his pocket, he looked into each of my eyes and then stuck a stethoscope to my chest. "Good. Now, take a few deep breaths."

I did as he instructed, and it felt like someone was trying to claw their way out of my chest. "Oh, that hurts like a—"

"Yes, I'm sure it does. You took a shotgun blast to the chest. Breathing deeply is going to hurt for several days, but you were quite fortunate."

"Fortunate? Really? I got shot with a twelve-gauge shotgun, and you call that fortunate?"

"No, not that whole getting shot part. I'm sure that sucked, but you were fortunate when the buckshot hit everything except the parts that would've killed you. It's a one-in-a-million chance. The angels above must want you alive for some reason. By all rights, you should be standing in front of Saint Peter having a conversation about going up or down, but you're still here."

"No, doc. You've got it all wrong. I'm not the kind of guy who's going to cure cancer or save the world. I'm just a bum who should be dead."

He lifted the clipboard from the foot of my bed. "Ah, so it's Millhouse. When you came in last night, you didn't have any ID on you, so you've been John Doe Number Three for the last several hours of your life."

"What about Linda?"

"I'm sorry, Mr. Millhouse. I don't know who that is."

"Linda's the woman who came in the same time as me last night. At least, I guess she came in at the same time. We were both shot during the robbery."

He shook his head. "I don't know anything about her. I'm the only cardiothoracic surgeon who was on overnight, so if she was shot like you, I would know about it."

"What if she was shot in the hand?" I was hopeful the nurse had been correct.

"I wouldn't know," he said. "That would be the ortho guys."

"When can I go?"

The doctor laughed. "Go? You were shot in the chest at close range with a twelve-gauge shotgun. I pulled eight buckshot pellets out of your chest cavity last night. You're going to be our guest for several days."

"Several days? What about my field jacket? When will I get that back? And I could really use a drink."

Dr. Blankenship had pity in his eyes. "I'm sorry, but I don't know anything about your jacket. We'll be moving you up to a room soon, and I'll tell the nurse to bring you something to drink. If you don't have any more questions for me, I'll check on you later this afternoon. The hospitalist will be making rounds as well."

When they rolled me into my room upstairs, I wasn't alone. A gentleman closing in on triple digits occupied a second bed. *The Price Is Right* was playing on the television mounted high on the wall opposite our beds.

It came as a disappointment when I learned Dr. Blankenship didn't tell the nurses I could have a drink. All they would bring was water in a pitcher and a ridiculous plastic sippy cup. They gave me medicine throughout the day and checked on me at regular intervals, but I drifted in and out of sleep, so keeping track of time was impossible.

I thought I must've been dreaming when I heard a disembodied voice say, "An attempted armed robbery at the Gateway Books and Gifts last night left two gunmen dead and two innocent victims wounded. Details coming up next."

Gateway Books? That's my bookstore. Are they talking about me?

I blinked against the harsh fluorescent light of the room as I tried to pull myself from unconsciousness. The news reporter said, "News Six has obtained exclusive footage of the deadly shootout that cost two armed robbers their lives at the hands of a, so far, unnamed good Samaritan. At just before eight o'clock last evening, two men armed with twelve-gauge shotguns entered the Gateway Books and Gifts on Magnolia Avenue, demanding the money from the registers. What the would-be robbers didn't count on was the reaction by one of the store's customers. The footage you are about to see was captured by the in-store security cameras. I must warn you the images are graphic in nature and may be disturbing for younger viewers or those sensitive to violence."

I watched the scene unfold on the screen, but I couldn't make myself understand what I was seeing. I knew the bearded, disheveled man in the video was me, but it felt like I was watching someone else. The footage had been edited to hide the actual impact of the shotgun blasts, but hearing the echoing reports of both weapons sent chills down my spine.

When the video ended, the reporter said, "The good Samaritan in the video has yet to be identified, but according to a spokesman for the Knoxville Police Department, the two deceased gunmen were David Wayne Shepherd of Powell, Tennessee, and Randy Kent Michaelson, also from Powell. Both men were on parole for previous crimes not involving firearms. Linda McCarter of Seymour, Tennessee, suffered a gunshot wound to her left hand and forearm but is reported to be in stable condition and expected to fully recover. The cashier, Lori Gail Smith of Knoxville, was unhurt, as was the store manager, Brenda Dawn McClean. Stay tuned to WATE-TV-6 for more details of this deadly, foiled armed-robbery attempt as they become available."

I lay motionless and in awe of what I saw and heard. I couldn't understand why I would've gotten involved and how I could've survived.

The curtain that had been obscuring my geriatric roommate slid shakily on its metallic track, and the old man lifted his head. "That guy looks just like you. Was that you? Are you the guy in that video?"

I stared at him for a long time, trying to determine my answer and if I'd tell him the truth. Finally, I said, "No...no, I don't think so."

"You don't think so? What do you mean you don't think so? It was either you or it wasn't, so which is it?"

"I don't know," I admitted. "I don't remember much about last night."

"For God's sake, son. Are you some kind of lunatic or something? How can you not know if that was you?" He pulled the curtain back into place and mumbled, "My word. They've put a crazy person in my room. Doesn't even know if it was him or not. Just what I need...a crazy person in my room."

As I lay in my bed trying to piece the whole scene together, a nurse wheeled Linda into my room. Her left hand and arm were in a bright pink cast. She rose from the wheelchair and approached me, tears streaming down her face. With her cast arm practically strapped to her body, the woman reached out with her right and hugged me as if I were her long-lost son. "You saved my life, John. I'll never be able to repay you. Are you okay?"

I stared at her in disbelief. "But I saw you get hit. How...?"

Laughing through her tears, she said, "Yeah, I got hit, but that's not what sent me to the floor. I guess it was too much for me, and I fainted. It's funny now, but I think I even peed a little."

Laughing felt good. I couldn't remember the last time I'd had a real belly laugh, although it only took a few seconds for my body to protest as agonizing bolts of electric pain surged through my chest and shoulders.

Note to self: no more laughing...ever.

The curtain came back. "It *was* you, you little scoundrel. I knew it was you."

"Shut up, old man. Can't you see I have a visitor?"

He yanked the curtain back into place. "I knew it was him. I just knew it. Crazy bastard, running into a gunfight like some kind of John Wayne or somebody. I knew it the whole time. I knew it."

Linda hugged me again, still crying. "I'm so glad you're going to be all right."

I didn't know what to say, so I said the only thing that came to mind. "I broke a coffee pot and a light bulb. I don't have any way to pay for them, but I'm sorry. Maybe I can do some work to make up for it."

Linda grinned. "Oh, John. You never have to worry about that. I've got a feeling you can break whatever you want in that store from now on and nobody will give a hoot. You're a hero. You're my hero."

I didn't like the word *hero*. It was for other people, but definitely not me. I was an alcoholic, homeless bum, and that's all I'd ever be.

"They took my field jacket with your muffins in the pockets, and nobody knows where it is. I need those muffins and that jacket. It's the only one I have."

She patted my arm and frowned. "There's no need for you to worry. The muffins were stale anyway, and I'll get you another jacket. Nobody's going to let you go hungry in here, so you just get better. I'm worried about you."

I didn't understand why Linda was worried. Maybe it was because she knew they'd give my cot away at the shelter if I didn't come back, and then I wouldn't have anywhere to sleep except back on the street again.

* * *

"Mr. Millhouse, I'm Dr. Bernstein. I'm the hospitalist assigned to your case. I'll be taking care of you while you're with us. Who is your primary care physician?"

I shook my head, and he made some notes.

"I see the nurses already asked you about family members, and you said you don't have any. Is that right?"

I didn't want to talk about my family. I was an embarrassment to them, so it was better if I pretended they didn't exist...just like they did to me. "Yeah, there's nobody," I mumbled.

"How about an address?"

I shook my head.

"Okay, so where do you live, Mr. Millhouse?"

"I sleep at the shelter by the bus station."

He made a few more notes. "Okay, how about medications, drugs of any kind—legal or otherwise—and any preexisting medical conditions?"

"I used to take antidepressants the VA gave me, but not anymore. I don't take drugs except for alcohol when I can get it. And yeah, I've got some preexisting medical conditions." I held up my scarred, twisted thumbs.

He leaned in, examining my hands. "What happened there?"

"I was tortured by a drug cartel in Colombia in ninety-two after they shot the tail boom off my helicopter. They stuck my hands through a wire fence and braced my thumbs together with metal clamps so I couldn't escape again. And I got shot in the chest with a shotgun two nights ago...or maybe it was last night."

Dr. Bernstein didn't write of my answers on his chart, but he did stare at me with his brow furrowed in disbelief. "I'm going to request a psychological consult. Do you know what that means?"

I slowly nodded. "Yeah, it means you think I'm crazy, and you're going to have one of your shrinks confirm your suspicions."

"No, that's not it at all, but if you're having hallucinations and delusions about helicopter crashes and being tortured by drug cartels, I think we probably need to get you back on some medication to clear your mind."

From behind the curtain, I heard, "I knew he was crazy. I knew it from the minute they rolled him in here. I knew it."

I glared at the doctor. "They're *not* hallucinations, and I'm not delusional. It's all in my file with Dr. Murphey at the VA hospital in Johnson City. Call him."

"Okay, Mr. Millhouse. I'll give Dr. Murphey a call and see what he has to say, but in the meantime, I'm going to ask one of my colleagues from psychiatry to come have a talk with you. Is that okay?"

It didn't matter if it was okay with me or not. The shrink was coming, and there was nothing I could do about it. "Do you know where my field jacket is? I need it."

"Try to get some rest. Do you need something to help you sleep?"

If he wasn't going to tell me where my field jacket was, I was finished answering his questions. He made a few more notes on my chart and stepped through the curtain to check on my ancient, clairvoyant roommate who wouldn't stop saying "I knew it."

When he'd finished behind the curtain, Dr. Bernstein emerged and tapped his hand on the footboard of my bed. "I'll see what I can do about finding your jacket, Mr. Millhouse."

I nodded my appreciation.

The scraping sound of the metallic hangers in the aluminum track grated on my nerves every time the old guy pulled on the curtains.

"Hey, Millhouse. That's your name, right? Millhouse?"

I turned my head to eye him.

"Yeah, I thought so," he said. "Anyway, why are you so worked up over that field jacket of yours? That's all you talk about is that damned field jacket and that malarkey about the drug cartel. What's wrong with you anyway?"

"Linda gave me three muffins. I ate one of them and put the other two in the pockets. It's the only jacket and the only muffins I've got, and now they're gone. What's it to you, anyway?"

He coughed as if he were going to hack up a kidney, then finally caught his breath. "Yeah, okay, I get that, but what about that drug cartel crap? Are you some kind of whacko or what?"

I glowered at the old man. "I'm not some kind of whacko. I was a helicopter pilot in the Army, and I got shot down in a Colombian jungle by some cocaine cowboys in ninety-two. I survived and escaped—twice actually—then I wrote a few books. And I used to teach English at UT."

The old man coughed and laughed simultaneously. "Yeah, right. I knew you were crazy. They'll be moving you up to the seventh floor loony bin as soon as the shrink sees you. And good riddance is what I say. When they haul you off, I'll finally be able to get some peace and quiet again."

I returned to my task of staring into the light above my bed and wishing I'd accepted Dr. Bernstein's offer of something to help me sleep. The pain meds would do the trick sooner or later, but I wanted sooner instead of later.

I drifted in and out for a few hours until I heard the same reporter's voice who'd shown the security camera footage of the bookstore.

"On our six o'clock broadcast, we showed you video of an unidentified good Samaritan intervening in an attempted armed robbery at the Gateway Books and Gifts on Magnolia Avenue last night. That good Samaritan has now been identified as Johnathon D. Millhouse, a former Army captain and helicopter pilot, as well as a former University of Tennessee English professor and novelist. Sources tell us Millhouse has been homeless for several years and most recently resided at the Christian Brotherhood Mission on Central Street in Knoxville."

I watched an image of who I used to be consume the screen. In the first picture, I was wearing my Army Class-A uniform, and the second picture was from the dust jacket of my novels.

The curtain didn't move, but I heard the old man say, "Well, I'll be damned. Maybe that whacko ain't as crazy as I thought."

CHAPTER 6
Two Boats and a Helicopter

University of Tennessee Medical Center
March 3, 2012

It was day number three, and I'd lost all hope of ever seeing my field jacket again. The old man behind the curtain was half right. The psychiatrist wanted to move me to the seventh floor—what the old guy called the loony bin—but there was no room. That left me stuck with the curmudgeon, and him stuck with the whacko.

"Hey, Millhouse. Are you awake?"

He'd stopped pulling the curtain back to talk to me. I guess he didn't mind talking to a whacko as long as he didn't have to look at one.

"Yeah, I'm awake. What is it?"

"So, all that stuff they're saying about you. Is it true?"

"What stuff?"

Another coughing fit preceded his hoarse, gravely attempt at communication. "Sorry, it's stage-four lung cancer. I can't do nothing about the coughing."

Several days was my sentence, but the old guy was doing life, spending his final days watching the news and *Price Is Right*.

"I'm sorry to hear that. Why won't you tell me your name?"

I could hear him trying to catch his breath. "You've never asked me my name."

"Well, I'm asking now."

"It's Ed. Ed Bowling. So, all that stuff about you being in the Army and being a professor...Is it true?"

"It used to be true, but that was a long time ago."

He cleared his throat. "I'm not going to live long enough to be subtle, so I'll just come out with it. What the hell happened? You were a pilot and a professor and a big-time writer, and then you end up in the charity ward pissed off about a field jacket and some old muffins. How does something like that happen?"

His question hit me harder than anything the shrinks had ever asked. I immediately went to work thinking up excuses and deciding who I could blame, but I finally settled on the truth. "I made a bunch of terrible decisions in a row and stepped off a cliff."

"It ain't too late, you know. You've still got time to turn it around."

I laughed. "Turn what around? I'm supposed to be the crazy one, old man, but it's starting to sound like you may be further off your rocker than me. I don't have anything to go back to. They'll never let me teach again. I can't fly anymore. Nobody's going to read anything I write, and I don't own anything...not even my field jacket. I've got nothing."

"Listen to me, young man. You've got the one thing you need to get everything else you want. You've got time, and as long as you've got time, everything else is possible. I'm trying to draw water out of a dry well over here. I'll be dead before spring, but not you. You cheated death at least twice already. If that crap about the helicopter and the cartel is true, you beat that ordeal, and you lived through getting shot. How many more boats and helicopters do you need?"

I stared at the curtain as if I could see through it. "Boats and helicopters?"

Ed yanked the curtain back. "Are you telling me you don't know the boats and helicopter story?"

"No, Ed. I don't know the boats and helicopter story."

He coughed and sat up in bed. "So, this guy, he was a good faithful Christian guy. You know the kind. He went to church all the time, did all the right stuff. A flood came, and the first floor of his house was underwater. A guy rows up in a boat and says, 'Hey, man. Get in the boat, and I'll take you to safety.' The guy says, 'Oh, no, the Lord will provide. I'll be fine.' The water keeps rising to the second floor, and a motorboat comes up. The guy in the boat says, 'Hey, man. Get in the boat, and I'll take you to safety,' but the dude says, 'No, the Lord will provide. I'll be fine.' Finally, the water keeps rising, and the guy's up on his roof. A helicopter flies up and lowers a rope ladder. The pilot yells out over the loudspeaker, 'Climb up, and I'll take you to safety.' The dude was all like, 'No, I'm good. The Lord will provide.' So, the water keeps rising, and the dude drowns and goes to Heaven, and he's real upset with God. He says to God, 'I trusted you to provide for me. What happened?' God said, 'I sent two boats and a helicopter. What more did you want?'"

I shook my head. "Ed, you've only got a little time left on Earth, and you just wasted two minutes telling me that stupid story."

"Maybe it was worth two minutes of whatever I've got left for you to *hear* that story. Maybe escaping from the jungle and surviving getting shot were your two boats. Don't pass up that helicopter when it comes."

"I think you belong on the seventh floor, you crazy old coot."

A familiar voice spoke from just outside the door. "Excuse me, but are you John Millhouse?"

I turned from crazy old Ed to see a beautiful young woman of maybe twenty-five standing in the door to our room. She had long, brown hair and a backpack across her shoulder.

"Yes, I'm John Millhouse. Who are you?"

There was something familiar about the woman. I knew her dimple and deep brown eyes, but I wasn't sure how I could know her. She was half my age, making her too young to have been one of my students, and too old to be any member of my family I didn't know. Besides, no one in my family would've shown up at the hospital to see me.

"I'm Anna," she said as she stepped through the door and unshouldered her backpack. "Do you mind if I come in?"

"You're already in, so what difference does it make if I mind?"

"Mr. Millhouse, if you'd rather I leave, I won't bother you, but I'd like to talk for a few minutes if you don't mind."

Ed started one of his coughing episodes that lasted longer than any I'd heard in the past three days.

Anna discreetly peeked around the curtain. "Is he okay?"

"Hey, Ed," I said. "This girl out here wants to know if you're okay. So, are you okay?"

"What girl?"

The way Anna lifted her chin, ever so slightly, reminded me of how my mother would stand in front of the oven waiting for the cookies to be just right.

"I don't know," I said. "Some girl named Anna."

Ed pulled back the curtain and peered at Anna. His eyes left the girl's face and focused on me, then back to her. He pulled the curtain back into place and mumbled, "That's weird."

I looked up at Anna. "I think he's okay. He's just old and grouchy."

She pointed toward the chair beside my bed. "Do you mind if I sit down for a few minutes?"

"Suit yourself," I said. "What do you want to talk about?"

She opened the flap on her backpack and pulled out my first novel. It was a paperback copy that looked as if it had been read four hundred times.

"I'm a grad student at UT, and when I found out you were here in the hospital, I couldn't believe it. I just had to come meet you. I know this is weird and all, but I've read everything you've ever written, and I think you're amazing."

I couldn't stop looking at Anna's eyes. They reminded me of someplace I wanted to be but could never go. I didn't understand why her face felt so much like everywhere I wanted to be all at the same time.

"I don't understand, Anna. I wrote that book fifteen years ago. How did you find it, and why would you carry it around with you? It's just a stupid book about a guy who—"

"Oh, I know what it's about, and it's amazing. I've read it a dozen times or more. I've read everything of yours. I don't get all of it, but it's deep. At least some of it is."

I frowned. "I think you're looking for something that isn't there. It's just a story about a guy who screws up everything he touches, but he wants to get it right."

Her eyes lit up. "Exactly! That's what's so great about it. Even though he knows he's going to screw everything up, he keeps trying. He doesn't give up. He's determined. It's like he knows there's something he's going to be great at, and he's going to keep searching 'til he finds it. Whatever it is."

I cast her a look of disbelief. "That's what you get from that book? A guy who believes he can do it even though he's a screw-up? That's what you get?"

She squeezed the tattered book as if it were her favorite doll. "Totally. That's exactly what I get. Isn't that what you meant when you wrote it?"

"No, not at all. It's a story about a hapless guy who stumbles into something good in spite of his ineptitude. It's a story about a town nobody's ever heard of and the people who don't care what the world is doing around them. They're determined to keep doing what they've always done to prove what's right is right, no matter what the rest of the world thinks."

She furrowed her brow. "What? That's not what this book is about at all."

"I think I know what the book is about. I wrote it, for God's sake."

"Yeah, well, you may have written it, but maybe you didn't know what you were writing. Maybe you were making a statement even *you* didn't know you were making. Maybe you're like George Orwell or something."

"That's ridiculous," I said. "There's no hidden meaning or secret code in that piece of crap. I wrote that in five or six weeks, and trust me when I tell you there was absolutely no deep thinking involved in the creation of that piece of trash."

Her mouth hung open, and she hugged the worn paperback to her chest like a frightened child. "Okay, well, I'll go and leave you alone. I'm glad you let me come in. Thank you."

I suddenly didn't want her to leave. "I'm sorry if I said something you didn't expect. It's just that I'm a different person than I was when I wrote that."

She slid the book back into her pack. "No, you're not. You're just different on the outside. That's all. The guy who wrote that book—a book that means so much to so many people—is still the same guy. Maybe you just won't admit it."

She wore the wisdom of age on the flesh of youth. The contrast made her something more than she was on the surface, and probably more than she'd ever let herself believe she could be.

I wanted to come up with some way to make her stay. I wanted to hear her voice and see her face a few more minutes, but I couldn't understand why. "Hey, before you go. What are you studying at UT?"

It was a wasted question. Her answer didn't matter. What mattered was the thirty seconds it would take her to tell me where her academic passion lay.

"English Literature," she said as if I should have known.

"English Lit? Who's your favorite poet?"

She smiled, and her dimple shone like a diamond in her cheek. "Walt Whitman, of course."

I had run out of questions, but I still didn't want her to leave, so I recited the only Whitman poem I could think of. "O Captain! my Captain! our fearful trip is done, The ship has weather'd every rack, the prize we sought is won, The port is near, the bells I hear, the people all exulting, While follow eyes the steady keel, the vessel grim and daring;"

She finished the first stanza. "But O heart! heart! heart! O the bleeding drops of red, Where on the deck my Captain lies, Fallen cold and dead."

We smiled and shared a silent, indescribable moment. Finally, when it had become too heavy for either of us, my roommate yanked the curtain back. "What the hell kind of poetry reading crap is going on over there?"

Ignoring the old man, Anna said, "So, do you think it might be okay if I came back tomorrow?"

"Suit yourself," I said. "I'll be here."

She tilted her head and smiled as if she knew a secret no one else knew. "Thanks, Mr. Millhouse. I'll see you tomorrow."

She left me feeling empty, as if she'd taken a part of me with her. As if she possessed a part of me, without which I'd never be whole. I longed for her return.

The curtain slid closed in Ed's forceful hand. "Yep, you missed the two boats, and there went your helicopter."

CHAPTER 7
Sum of All Sins

VA Hospital, Johnson City, TN
1994

"John, I think you may have the wrong impression of what the medication is supposed to accomplish. It doesn't erase our past. It merely allows us to compartmentalize things that would otherwise overwhelm our minds. The medication allows us to deal with things individually. Without it, we feel as though we're trying to drink from a firehose. Everything seems unmanageable until we learn to face one issue at a time and continue to function in society."

Dr. Murphey's explanation was unnecessary, but I let him keep talking in hopes that I wouldn't have to confess my ever-torturing sin.

"I understand, doc, but this isn't the kind of thing I can face and put behind me. I think I'm stuck with this one."

I could see the hesitation on his face. We were seventy-five minutes into a ninety-minute session, and he didn't want to dive into my black water with only fifteen minutes remaining before the next screwed-up combat vet stumbled through the door.

Dr. Murphey never wore a watch during our sessions; instead, he kept an eye on a clock behind his patients. That was a brilliant piece of deception on his part. If he glanced at his watch throughout a session, it would be easy for me and other patients to feel he was more concerned with the time than with helping us deal with our demons.

"You're worried about the time, aren't you, doc?"

He smirked. "I'm glad all my patients aren't as smart as you, John. We have less than fifteen minutes left, but I think it's important we talk about what's going on with you. If you'll excuse me for just a minute. Can I get you anything?"

"I'm not sure I want to—"

He held up one finger. "Just give me a minute, John. I'll be right back."

Presumably, he postponed his next patient. Doing so told me he took my problem more seriously than the poor sap's in the waiting room. I wondered if that meant I was worse than the next guy, or if Dr. Murphey just couldn't wait to hear me divulge my sum of all sins.

He settled into his wingback chair. "All right. I'm sorry about that."

My mouth turned to cotton as I thought about coming clean. I'd never told anyone what I'd done. I didn't even want to admit it to myself, and I was on the verge of spilling my guts to a government doctor. I didn't feel good about that, but Dr. Murphey had helped with my other issues, and he'd returned the gift of sleep to my life. If anyone could absolve me of my guilt, self-loathing, and disgust over my deed, maybe it was him. That's what I wanted to believe, but absolution wasn't in the cards for me that day.

"So, I guess you want me to tell you what I did."

He shook his head. "No, John. I don't want you to tell me what you did. I want you to tell me about the last time you spent an entire day not thinking about whatever it is you did. I want to talk about it. Do you remember the last time you had a day like that?"

If he was trying to knock me off balance, he'd done it. I felt like I'd stepped into the ring with Muhammad Ali, and I was on the verge of falling victim to his rope-a-dope.

"I guess it was right after I did it. I mean, I didn't think a lot about it for a few weeks, or maybe even a couple of months, and then it started eating at me. Now, it seems like the more time passes, the more it haunts me."

He leaned toward me, seeming to focus on my lips as I spoke. "Why do you use the word *haunt* to describe how you feel about what happened?"

"That's not the right word, doc."

He scowled. "Do you mean *haunt* isn't the right word?"

I shook my head. "No, *haunt* is definitely the right word. *Happened* isn't the right word. It didn't *happen*. I did it. *Happen* implies an occurrence beyond anyone's control. Volcano eruptions *happen*. Hurricanes *happen*. This didn't *happen*. I committed this unthinkable act. Nothing about it just *happened*."

He probed at the flesh of his jaw with the tip of his tongue. "It's healthy to take responsibility for things we've done, but it is possible to take too much responsibility sometimes. Perhaps what you're feeling is entirely self-imposed and far less vile than you seem to believe."

"I'd been in Colombia for almost a full month when the Delta operators showed up. For the first couple of weeks I was there, before the Delta guys came, I never knew where or why we were going to fly. I just went where they told me, but when Delta showed up, that all changed."

Dr. Murphey crossed his legs and sat back in his chair. That's when I realized I was telling the story for the first time. Part of me wanted to stop. I could stand up, walk out, and never come back, but something inside me kept me on that couch. Something kept me talking.

"Instead of flying where they told me, I planned the strike mission with Delta and the DEA special agent in charge. It was an insertion, strike, and exfiltration mission. I'd drop the six Delta operators about a kilometer north of the cocaine production site. They'd hump in, take out the site, and haul ass to the rendezvous point, where I'd pluck them out of the jungle and fly them back to camp." I paused, realizing the egregious violation of op-sec I was committing. "Doc, this is still classi-fied, so I'm not supposed to be talking about it."

"John, it's okay. You told me whatever you did happened after you got back to the States. Nothing you did when you came home is classified."

I grimaced. "Yeah, but to understand what I did, you have to know what happened down there...before I came home."

"Okay. What we discuss here stays between us. I'm required by law to keep anything you tell me in the strictest confidence unless it places you or someone else at risk for bodily harm or death, or, of course, if there's a threat to national security. Outside of those conditions, any-thing you tell me will never leave this room."

His reassurance apparently convinced my mind it was okay to tell the whole story, and I kept talking. "So, Delta guys are usually standoffish, but this team was different. They'd been together for a while, and for some reason, they took me in. I drank beer with them at night, and we talked about people we knew in common. I got to know a couple of the guys pretty well. I was an outsider, not being Special Forces or Delta, but they let me into their circle anyway. One of the guys, Payne Hollenbeck —I'll never forget his name—talked a lot about his family and how much he missed them. He had a boy and a girl, and they were trying for more. We weren't supposed to have pictures of our families on a mis-sion, but that didn't stop Payne. He showed me pictures of his wife and kids a dozen times. His wife was the homecoming queen and all that, and his kids were just beautiful. It was going to be his last mission. He was getting out of the Army and going back to Muscle Shoals to raise his family. 'Ain't nothin' more important than family, sir.' That's what he told me every time he talked about going home."

My mouth was turning to cotton again, and Dr. Murphey noticed. "Here, John. Have some water."

I took the bottle from his hand and drank it down. "So, the night of the mission came. We did everything at night because the Delta guys liked the cover of darkness, and our night-vision gear was top-shelf. We took off from camp a few minutes after midnight and headed up the mountain. I was pushing the chopper as hard as she'd go, and we were screaming along, right on top of the trees. That jungle canopy looks like the ground from above. It's dense and solid. The LZ was barely big enough to put a chopper in, but there was no room for error. An LZ is a landing zone, in case you didn't know."

He smiled. "Yes, I know."

"Yeah, I guess you would. Anyway, we'd practiced it a couple dozen times in a roped-off clearing that was eighty percent of the actual size of the LZ, so once I could do it in the practice area, the real thing would be a piece of cake. The LZ came into sight, and I yelled over my shoulder to the Delta guys in the back, 'We'll be on deck in two minutes!' That's when I saw the first RPG, which is a—"

Dr. Murphey nodded. "Yes, I know. A rocket-propelled grenade."

"Yeah, well, that first one was dead on my nose, and there was nowhere to go but down. I shoved the stick forward, dumped the collective, and stuck the skids in the jungle canopy, but thankfully, I kept the rotors clear. I pulled up and banked out to the right, hoping to duck over the edge of a ridgeline to put a few billion tons of earth and trees between us and the grenadiers, but we were heavy, full of fuel, gear, and operators, so the chopper didn't respond like I wanted. It was sluggish in the heat and high altitude of the mountains. I got the tail low, and it got sloppy. I have to hand it to those Delta guys, though. They kept their wits about them and started pouring fire into the jungle while I wrestled with the controls of the helicopter. The thing finally started flying again, and I got the nose pushed over enough to get some forward speed. That's when the sky lit up like a Christmas tree. RPGs were everywhere.

I never saw the one that actually got us, but I knew immediately when it happened. The pedals went dead, and we started spinning like a top. The tail rotor was gone. I didn't know it at the time, but the whole tail boom was gone. That scenario is deadly when you've got a million acres of clear ground beneath you, but when you're ten feet over the jungle, there's almost no way to survive it."

The passive, distant look the doctor typically wore was gone, replaced by a look of fear and anticipation. He was in that doomed chopper with me. I could see it in his eyes.

"I made the decision to stick us in the trees. We had a better chance of surviving if I could let the chopper settle into the canopy and put the Delta guys on the ground. They're some of the best in the world at gunfights, so if I could keep us alive long enough to get their boots on the ground, we had a shot at getting out of that jungle alive. We hit the trees a lot harder than I wanted, and two of the guys fell out of the door. If they survived the fall, they'd be little more than a pile of broken bones when they hit the ground. When the rotor hit the trees, it was like trying to swim inside a blender."

The doctor was out of his legs-crossed pose and leaning in.

"When all the pieces stopped moving, I thought for two seconds we might've survived, but then I smelled the fire. The chopper was going up in flames, and we had to get out. My door was jammed, so I went through the hole where the windshield used to be. Strapped to my body was a Beretta M-9 9mm and a Ka-Bar fighting knife. To say the least, I was not prepared to fight off an army of coked-up Colombians. I saw the guys crawling from the burning chopper behind me, and everybody was hurt, but none of us knew how badly as we moved away and took cover. Of the six Delta operators, three had survived. My copilot—a DEA pilot named Chicken Foot—was dead when we hit the trees."

"Chicken Foot?"

"Yeah, Chicken Foot. That's what we called him. I never knew his real name until I got home. Payne was still alive, along with a guy named Schwartz and a young operator named Billings. The kid, Billings, was pretty scared, but he wasn't the only one. I was terrified, but I didn't have any choice but to keep it together. I was the highest-ranking man still alive. That meant I was in charge."

I paused long enough to drain another bottle of water.

"Payne shoved a rifle toward me and said, 'You're gonna need this, Cap. Keep your head down, and kill anything that moves. Which direction is the highest ground?' I pointed straight ahead, and that seemed to satisfy him. Then he spoke the words I'll never forget: 'If you don't make it, we'll do our best to drag you out of here. If we don't make it, tell our kids we were brave.'"

"They didn't make it. Schwartz and Billings died while we were shooting our way toward the river. Being outnumbered like that, there was no way we could get to high ground, so the river was our best option to escape. During the fight, Payne took one in the thigh and one in the upper arm. He wasn't dead, but he wasn't mobile. There was no way I could carry him, and I couldn't leave him behind. It didn't take long for us to shoot up all the ammo we carried into the jungle. That left us sitting ducks. There was nothing left for us to do but accept our fate. I got things right with God and prepared myself for the next bullet that had to be only seconds away. But instead of killing Payne and me, they took us. A bullet would've been better. Payne bled to death before the sun came up, and they tortured me so I would divulge the location of our camp, equipment, and personnel numbers. I never told 'em a thing, and I eventually escaped...twice. The second time I ran for my life, knowing they'd never let me live if I was caught. I made it to the river, and eventually, the GPS tracker sewn into my shirt led the other flight crew right to me. They picked me up, and I was back in camp less than seventy-two hours after the ordeal had begun. Shortly after that, I was headed back to the States."

The doctor looked flabbergasted. "That's an incredible story, John. That's enough to terrify anyone for the rest of his life. You have no reason to be ashamed of anything."

I huffed. "I have every reason to be ashamed. I should've banked instead of diving. We might've been able to get the hell out of Dodge if I hadn't stuck the skids in the top of those trees."

"You can't know that. You did the best you could. You did the best *anyone* could've done in those circumstances."

I took a long, deep breath. "All of that is bad, and I'll never get over it, but what came next was far worse."

"Tell me," he said. "And take all the time you need."

"When we got back to the States, I made the rounds. I personally went to see the widows and families of every one of the men I'd gotten killed that night."

"John, you can't hang that around your neck. You didn't get them killed. The Colombians killed them. Not you."

I closed my eyes. "Yeah, but I was in charge, so those men were my responsibility. Anyway, I consciously saved Payne's wife and family until the end. Telling them what happened and apologizing would be the hardest thing I'd ever have do. I phoned to let them know I was coming, and in hindsight, I wish I hadn't made that call. If I had just shown up and knocked on their door, I would've never done what I did. Doc, this is the part that's hard to talk about."

"It's okay. Take your time. I assure you, getting it off your chest is the first step in dealing with it."

I ran my fingers through my hair as I gathered my thoughts. "Sherry Hollenbeck answered the door. Seeing her in person was like meeting someone I'd known for years. Payne's pictures of his family and hearing him talk about how much he wanted to be home with them made me feel like I'd known the whole family all along. I introduced myself, and Sherry invited me in, tears streaming down her face. I'd practiced my speech a hundred times, but I couldn't recall a word of it.

"I sat down on the edge of the sofa and told her the whole story of what happened, making sure she knew how much Payne loved her and the kids. She listened in silence with tears continually pouring from her eyes. When I finished, I asked her where the children were, and she told me they weren't ready to hear what really happened to their daddy.

"When I stood to leave, Sherry stood, hugged me, and thanked me for coming in person instead of sending a letter like the Army did. I returned her hug and reassured her that I felt she deserved to know the truth, and that it was only right she heard it face-to-face. When our embrace ended, she kept her arms around my waist and looked up into my eyes. She was beautiful in spite of the emptiness and desperation on her tear-stained face. After the tears stopped coming, she slid her hand behind my neck and pulled my lips to hers in a long, desperate kiss. I have no idea why I didn't pull away. I'll never know, but what happened in the hours that followed is the worst thing I'll ever do. It was the worst thing anyone could ever do. I'll never forgive myself, and I'll never be able to medicate it away."

CHAPTER 8
Crazy Old Man

University of Tennessee Medical Center
March 4, 2012

"Hey, Ed. Are you awake?"

Ed had stopped closing the curtain between us. Perhaps he thought he might miss something exciting, but when he wasn't watching TV, it was impossible to tell if he was awake. The man rarely moved or made any sounds other than a coughing event several times every hour.

"Yeah, I'm awake. I was just thinking about a girl I knew in Spain after the war."

"Which war?" I asked.

"Hell, I don't remember. What do you want?"

How does he not remember which war?

I almost laughed but remembered how badly laughing hurt, so I stifled it. "Do you remember that college girl who came in here yesterday? Anna?"

"Yeah, sure. Your helicopter," he said, followed immediately by three minutes of coughing. He collected himself and wiped his mouth. "What about her?"

It broke my heart to see him hurting so badly after every coughing episode. "I was just trying to figure out why you called her my 'helicopter.'"

He shook his head. "Oh, for God's sake, kid. Open your eyes. You got nobody, right?"

His question stung a little, and I didn't answer, but he was right.

"That's what I thought. So, this girl comes in here. Obviously, she saw that crap on the news about you at the bookstore, and she's some kind of library freak and wanted to meet you. To her, you're a big deal or something. Who else you got in your life who thinks you're a big deal, huh?"

I still didn't answer, but that didn't slow him down.

"So, maybe surviving that crap in the jungle and then not getting killed the other night in the bookstore were your two boats, and you ignored them. Now, maybe that girl—what's her name—is your godsend helicopter. I'm just saying you should've talked to her. That's all. It might've been good to have somebody help you remember when you had more to live for than a couple of stale muffins stuffed in a pocket of a ratty old field jacket."

He may have had more to say, but the coughing returned, and with it came a lot of blood. I slammed the rail of my bed down and jabbed at the nurse call button with my deformed thumb. Pulling myself out of the bed, I moved as quickly as I could to Ed's side. I held the old man's head in my arms and tried to keep him sitting up. With that much blood, he'd choke to death or drown if he lay back down.

"Nurse! Somebody! Get in here!" I yelled, but nobody came.

With Ed still in my arms, I pressed the button that brought the bed into a sitting position. When I believed I could lean his body against the head of the bed and keep him from drowning in his own blood, I shuffled for the door and into the hallway.

"Somebody help! He's dying."

Dr. Bernstein, the hospitalist, came out of a room several doors down the hall and looked up when I yelled. He turned away and ordered a nurse to bring something, but I couldn't understand what he was saying. I didn't care as long as he helped Ed. The doctor began running toward me.

I stepped out of the way and pointed toward my dying roommate. "He's coughing up a lot of blood."

A pair of nurses pushing a cart came down the hall at the same pace as the doctor. I stayed back to give them plenty of space and then followed them back into the room.

Dr. Bernstein was feeling for Ed's pulse in his neck. With the nurses still rushing toward the dying man, the doctor turned and slowly shook his head. "Time of death, seven-forty-two a.m."

I'd known the man for less than three full days, but watching him lose his battle with the cancer that had ravaged his body left me with a lump in my throat and a new pain in my gut. For the first time in more years than I could remember, I felt the emptiness of missing another human being. I'd come to like Ed in spite of his grouchiness and endless need to have the television blaring night and day.

A team of people dressed in scrubs rolled Ed away, and another pair of men cleaned every speck of evidence that Ed Bowling had ever occupied the room. Within twenty minutes of his death, a new bed was rolled in, and the room, like me, was half empty.

At 8:15, the breakfast guy showed up with two trays. Seeing me sitting in the chair, he rolled the table in front of me and placed one of the trays on the Formica top. He motioned toward the empty bed. "Did Mr. Bowling expire?"

"Expire?" I said, incredulously. "Is that what you call it when somebody dies in this place? Expire?"

He looked at me as if he couldn't understand why I didn't approve of the word, and his nonchalance over Ed's death made my blood boil.

"What's wrong with you, man? He was a human being, for God's sake, not a carton of milk. People don't expire. People die. And Ed

Bowling died less than half an hour ago. Don't you people have any respect for anything around here?"

I was getting louder and more agitated with every word, and the disbelief and shock on the guy's face told me I was pushing the issue too far, but I didn't care. I lifted the metal lid from my breakfast plate with every intention of hurling it at the man's head, but a voice from the doorway stopped me.

"Is everything okay in here, Mr. Millhouse?"

I turned to see Anna, the college girl from the day before, her eyes shifting wildly between the breakfast guy and me. I was mad, he was stupefied, and Anna looked shocked and disappointed. I was instantly ashamed and lowered the metal lid to the table.

The guy timidly approached, placed Ed's tray on my table, and backed away toward the door. "You can have his breakfast, man. I didn't mean to upset you. I was just—"

Anna placed her hand on his arm. "It's okay. I'm sure he didn't mean to yell at you."

He disappeared into the hallway, and Anna tossed her backpack onto my bed. "What's going on? You seem pretty upset."

I motioned toward the empty half of the room. "Ed passed away this morning."

A look of sadness overtook her beautiful young face, and I suddenly felt as if I'd seen that sadness before—as if I'd caused that sadness before.

"I'm so sorry," she said. "I don't know what to say."

"There's nothing you can say. I didn't even know him really. I was just upset because the breakfast guy asked me if Ed had expired. Can you believe that? He actually said the word *expired*."

She nodded. "Yeah, that's the word they use now. I don't like it either. It's like people are just jugs of milk or something."

Hearing her use the same analogy I'd used caught me off guard.

She pulled a chair from Ed's side of the room and sat across the table from me. Then she eyed the second tray of food. "Do you think they'd mind if I had whatever that is? I didn't have time for breakfast this morning."

I lifted the lid and slid Ed's plate toward her. "I don't think they'd mind at all, and to tell you the truth, I'd like to have the company. I've not had breakfast with anybody in a long time." I suddenly felt self-conscious about my beard and hair, and subconsciously ran my fingers through them.

She must have noticed. "My mom was a beautician, and I learned to do hair by watching her. Once, I even got in trouble for cutting my doll's hair." She waved her hand toward the mass of hair consuming my head. "I can come back later and see what I can do with all of that. We could have you looking like George Clooney in no time."

I didn't know what to say. Why did this girl want to cut my hair? What could she have possibly wanted from me?

"We were talking about you right before he died." I don't know why that popped out of my mouth, but there was nothing I could do about it. I secretly hoped she didn't hear me.

"Me?" she said, surprised. "Why would you two be talking about me?"

In a ham-fisted effort to change the subject, I said, "He and I talked about all sorts of things. Your name came up. That's all."

She smiled curiously. "Really? And what were you saying about me?"

I glanced toward the empty bed. "Actually, it was Ed who was doing the talking. He was old and sick. You know how the mind starts to go and people say ridiculous things."

Her smile continued. "Tell me. I want to know what he said, even if it was crazy."

I tried to decide whether to tell her the truth or make something up. I think she figured out what I was doing.

She leaned forward and caught my eyes with hers. "Don't lie to me, or I'll know."

"Oh, you will, huh? Are they teaching the art of lie-detecting at UT now?"

She shook her head. "Nope. I learned that little trick from my mom, too."

"Your mom sounds like quite a woman. Beautician, lie detector, and apparently a pretty good mom."

"Yeah, she's all that and more, but stop trying to change the subject. What was Ed saying about me?"

I settled on the truth...mostly. "He said he thought you might be good for me."

She tilted her head. "How so?"

"Oh, I've fallen on hard times the last few years, and, well, you can tell by looking at me I'm not the guy on the back cover of your book anymore. Ed thought maybe having a bright, young English student around might make me feel better."

She took a bite of something that was supposed to be scrambled eggs. "Yeah? And what do you think?"

I swallowed a mouthful of lukewarm coffee and smiled a little. "Ah, he was a crazy old man. What does he know?"

We ate breakfast in silence for the next few minutes, and even though we didn't talk, it was nice having somebody sitting across the table. It was nice to do something normal people do. I guess most people take things like that for granted, but when common things aren't common anymore, they tend to grow into uncommonly meaningful things, even for a bum like me.

Anna looked at her fancy digital watch. "I have to get going, but how about that trim this afternoon?"

I smiled behind a bramble of gray, stringy facial hair.

"I'll take that as a yes, mister. See you around four thirty." She slung her bag over her shoulder and headed for the hallway, but stopped in the door. "Thanks for breakfast. It was nice."

She danced away, and I couldn't stop thinking that maybe crazy old Ed wasn't so crazy after all.

* * *

Mostly out of boredom and clinging to the routine my life had taken on, I left the TV on louder than necessary and tuned to reruns of *The Price Is Right*.

Loneliness comes in all sorts of flavors. When I stopped taking the antidepressants and started drinking again, I blamed it on a type of loneliness that is purely imaginary and self-induced. I let myself believe I was the only person with darkness inside himself. Everyone around me had families and careers that seemed to fulfill them, and I had those things to some degree, but I wasn't fulfilled. Maybe I was fulfilled as long as the sun was in the sky, but when night fell upon me, the men I'd left behind in the jungle cried out, and the unthinkable atrocity of sleeping with the widow of my friend, a man who'd died fighting alongside me in the mountains of Colombia, was more than I could endure. I deserved to be rotting in that jungle, and Payne should've survived and come home to his beautiful wife and children. I wasn't meant to be alive. It was all wrong. By surviving, I'd somehow warped the reality that should have been. I deserved the agony those memories unleashed upon me every night. The life I led at the university and as a novelist was a lie. I was nothing more than a possessed carcass masquerading as a successful, well-adjusted member of society. The lies I was forced to tell the world had become nearly as heavy as the truths that tormented me. I turned from the antidepressants because I didn't want the relief they delivered. I didn't deserve that peace and pardon.

* * *

Dr. Bernstein arrived with a flock of medical students in tow and muted the television. I was lost in the memory of stepping off the ledge, and I forgot the TV was on.

Who won the showcase showdown, and did they guess within a hundred dollars and win both packages? I missed Bob Barker reminding everyone to have their pets spayed or neutered. That was my favorite part, and I missed it.

Dr. Bernstein opened every visit with the same question. "Mr. Millhouse, how are you feeling?"

"I miss Ed," I said before I'd given the words any thought. That left me in near panic. Bernstein wasn't asking about my mental state; he wanted to know how I was healing from the surgery. In a desperate effort to recover, I ran my hands over my chest and abdomen. "Much better. I think I'm ready to get out of here."

He appeared to ignore my comment and patted my bed with his palm. "How about you sit up here and pull your gown down so we can have a look?"

He'd phrased it in the form of a question, but it was a direction, not a request. Eying the medical students warily, I did as Dr. Bernstein asked. One by one, he removed the bandages and invited the soon-to-be doctors to have a look.

One particularly timid young lady approached with great trepidation, as if I might sink my teeth into her at any moment. As she leaned in to examine the worst of my eight entry wounds, I whispered, "I used to be a doctor. You could end up just like me."

I don't know why I did it. Perhaps it was an act of self-amusement or purely the behavior of a lunatic. Regardless, I immediately regretted saying it when the poor girl leapt back and gasped.

Bernstein was amused. "What is it, Dr. Lindon?"

"He said he was a doctor."

Dr. Bernstein tried to hold back his smile. "Did he also tell you he's a *New York Times* Best-Selling author?"

The confused young woman looked up at her mentor and frowned deeply. "No. Why would he say that?"

"Because both are true, Dr. Lindon, but neither is relevant to this case. Learning to separate the factual from the pertinent is sometimes the hardest part of our job."

Bernstein had taken an act of belligerence on my part and turned it into a teaching moment. I was impressed.

"Okay, Dr. Millhouse, you may pull your gown back up. Your wounds are healing far better than expected, and there's no sign of infection."

I hadn't been called Dr. Millhouse in over a decade, and although I'd earned the title, it was purely academic. I could explain the works of Poe, Milton, and Dickens, but I had no power to heal like the horde of young medical doctors gathered around Bernstein.

"So, does that mean I can go?" I asked.

Dr. Bernstein scratched his chin. "No, I'm afraid not. We'll be moving you up to the seventh floor this afternoon. They have a bed for you now.

"But I can't leave this room until after four thirty."

The doctor looked confused. "What do you mean, Mr. Millhouse?"

"I mean I can't leave this room until Anna comes back. She won't be able to find me, and she's going to cut my hair."

The med students mumbled, and a few even laughed. They knew what being moved to the seventh floor meant, and they knew I was insane. Especially Dr. Lindon.

Dr. Bernstein glowered at his students. "Wait for me in the hallway."

When his students left the room, he turned back to me. "For the record, I don't think you're crazy. I think you have a lot of demons, and I think you're on the verge of overcoming them—most of them, anyway—so I'll make sure you aren't moved upstairs until after you've seen Anna."

CHAPTER 9
Shave and a Haircut

I was going to the loony bin, and short of running for my life, there didn't seem to be anything I could do about it. For the homeless, the passage of time happens much differently than for those with careers, families, and schedules. I had nothing to look forward to in my life. I'd never declare, "Honey, I'm home," and hug my kids at the door after a long day at the office. I'd never take a vacation to Panama City Beach and build sandcastles with my sunburned toddlers. My life was endless minutes accumulating into dreadful hours, punctuated by shivering nights and hunger pang-filled days. I couldn't remember the last time I'd looked forward to anything...until March 4, 2012.

Anna, the determined college girl, would be back at 4:30, and I couldn't wait. It didn't make sense for me to be excited to see her, and it made even less sense that she wanted to keep coming back. People don't do things without motivations, but I couldn't come up with a reasonable explanation for her visitations. Maybe she thought I still had book royalties coming and she wanted to find a way to hustle me out of that money. Nothing else made sense.

Minutes passed like hours as the clock hands appeared to freeze in position. When 4:30 came and went, I knew it was too good to be true. She wasn't coming back. My day had consisted of losing Ed before breakfast, twenty minutes with Anna, and then six months waiting for her to return—at least that's how it felt. I would spend the remainder of my day committed to the psych ward, but at least I wouldn't be cold when the sun went down.

I didn't own anything, not even my field jacket, so there was nothing to pack. There was a clean gown and socks every morning, but even those weren't mine. They belonged to the hospital. Maybe the plastic sippy cup and Styrofoam water pitcher were mine, but I couldn't be certain.

At 4:42, I pushed the call button on my bed and waited for the impatient tone of whoever was at the other end of the line.

"Yes, Mr. Millhouse. What do you need?"

Now, there was an interesting question. What did I truly need? Food, shelter, clothing, and medical care. My needs were being met. When I pressed the button, it had been my intention to tell the nurse I was ready to move up to the seventh floor, but her question caught me off guard. What did I need?

"I need to see Anna. Have you seen her? She was supposed to be here at four thirty."

"I'm sorry, Mr. Millhouse. No one has asked to see you."

I could understand that. After all, who would want to see me?

"Oh, wait a minute. Here she comes, I think. Brunette around twenty years old?"

"Yeah, that's her," I said, certain I sounded far more excited than I should have.

Anna came skidding through the door. "I'm so sorry I'm late. I had to go get my stuff, and my car is a piece of crap."

Seeing her felt better than anything I'd known in years. I pretended to look at a watch that wasn't on my wrist. "It's fine. I didn't even realize you were late. Besides, it's not like I'm going anywhere."

Her smile lit up the room. "I know, but if I tell you I'll be here at four thirty, it's rude to be late."

I chuckled. "Did your mom teach you that?"

"Yeah, I guess so."

"Punctuality is important when you're part of polite society in the South. I don't think I'm part of anything, really."

She said so much without opening her mouth. The expressions on her face made it perfectly clear what was going on behind her dark eyes.

"Don't look at me like that. I don't want you to feel sorry for me." I pointed at the black pouch in her hand. "Is that what you're going to use to make me look like George Clooney?"

She held up the pouch. "It is. These are my mom's clippers and scissors and stuff."

I smiled. "If you're going to make me look like a movie star, you'll need a bigger bag than that."

She giggled. "Never underestimate what a good Southern girl can accomplish with a set of clippers and a comb. Now, let's get you in a chair."

She went to work on my unruly mop of black and gray hair and beard. Having someone touch me was, at first, a little uncomfortable. It had been so long since I'd felt anyone's hands on me. People tend to go to great lengths to avoid touching people like me. We're grungy and dirty, and perhaps people fear homelessness is a communicable disease. The nurses and doctors had touched me over the previous few days, but their hands-on contact had been through latex gloves and were requirements of their jobs. Anna was unselfconsciously pulling her fingers through my hair and lopping off massive clumps.

She started with my beard, although it was impossible to determine where the beard ended and the hair began. My hair fell to the barber cloth she'd placed around my shoulders and then slid to the floor at my feet. I tried to remember how my face had looked before I stopped caring, but that day was so far in my past that it was impossible for my mind to return there.

She pulled the scissors away from my hair and tilted her head. "Does that hurt?"

I looked up at her. "No, it doesn't hurt at all."

"How long has it been since you've had a haircut?"

I shrugged, unsure if I remembered a haircut before that one.

"Well, don't you worry. We'll have you looking like a brand-new man before you know it."

"Why are you doing this? What do you want from me?" The words tumbled from my tongue before I could stop them, and I sat terrified as Anna suddenly stopped what she was doing. I should've kept my mouth shut and let her work, but people don't volunteer to groom a homeless bum for no reason. She had to have a motive. Everyone has a motive.

"Can't a person just want to do something nice sometimes?"

Her response made me think of Dr. Murphey, who seemed to lack the ability to form a question without making it sound like a statement. Anna represented the other side of that coin. She delivered her answers as questions.

"Maybe some people can," I said, "but in my experience, people usually want something in return. I don't have anything to offer you."

I heard the resignation in her tone. "Okay, maybe I do want something."

I knew it.

She laid her clippers and comb on the table where we'd eaten breakfast and walked around in front of me. Bending down so we were eye to eye, she said, "I do want something from you, but I'd cut your hair even if you said no."

I wasn't sure I believed her, but something in the sincerity of her voice and the honesty in her dark eyes made me want to believe she was telling the truth.

"I want you to read my manuscript."

"Your manuscript?"

Shyness overtook honesty, and she dragged the toe of her shoe through a pile of hair at my feet. "Yes, my manuscript. I want to be a writer, like you."

Her declaration stung me to my core. I remembered the day I told Dr. Murphey I wanted to write. That longing to sculpt a story out of mere words and draw a reader into a world I created had once burned inside me the way it was now flaming inside Anna. My fire had long before smoldered and turned to cold, gray ash.

"You mean, a writer like I *used* to be."

She pulled a small towel from across her shoulder and brushed hair from my nose and around my eyes. "Is a baseball player on injured reserve still a baseball player?"

"What are you talking about? What do you know about baseball?"

The dimple on her left cheek came alive as she smiled. "He's still a baseball player. He just got hurt, and he's going through some stuff until he's ready to get back on the field. Right?"

She picked up her tools and set about working her way through the briars and brambles on my face and head. "You're an English professor, Dr. Millhouse, and a brilliant writer. You've just been off the field for a while. So, will you do it?"

What is she asking me? Does she want me to go back to teaching and writing?

"Will I do what?"

"Read my manuscript, silly. What did you think I meant?"

Can that really be all she wants?

"What's it about?" I asked.

Her answer surprised me more than her question.

Through a thoughtful, curious look, she said, "I don't know yet."

"What do you mean you don't know? How can you not know what your own manuscript is about?"

"I know the story, but books are not about the story they tell. They're about an underlying truth hidden inside the author. The story is just a method of delivery, a sugarcoating to make the bitter truth go down easier. I think of it like food."

"Food?"

"Yeah, like food. Its real purpose is to put fuel in our body, and it doesn't matter how that fuel gets inside of us. We have to get it, or we'll die. We dress it up and make it taste good, but the flavors and presentation are just ways to deliver the fuel to make people like it. I think that's what books are. They reveal something from deep inside the author, but they do it in a way that feels good when people read it."

She hesitated, and I couldn't tell if she was waiting for a reaction from me or if she was thinking about how to continue. It must have been the latter.

"At least, that's what I think. Maybe I'm wrong, but that's why I say I don't know what my manuscript is about. I know the story, but I haven't figured out what it is I'm trying to tell the world."

I remembered those days. I remembered when I believed I had something meaningful and powerful to say that would change the world forever. I was her a long time ago: ambitious, optimistic, and delusional. I wanted to tell her she'd grow out of that irrational, change-the-world delusion, but I said the last thing I expected to come out of my mouth. "I'd love to read your manuscript."

She threw her arms around me from behind and hugged me like a child who'd gotten exactly what she wanted for Christmas. I gasped in pain as she squeezed me, putting pressure on the wounds in my chest.

"I'm so sorry. I didn't mean to hurt you. I forgot—."

"It's fine," I breathed. "I'm just a little sore, that's all."

"I know. I just got excited. Let's finish your makeover."

"Makeover?" I said.

"*Transformation* might be a better word."

The pile of hair at my feet kept growing, and I couldn't imagine how I looked with that much hair missing. When the vibrating hum of the clippers finally fell silent, Anna smeared shaving cream over my face and the back of my neck. The smell and feel of the warm foam on my skin was a sensation I'd long forgotten.

When she finished the shave, she stood back and smiled. "Go have a look."

I raised my hands to my face and felt the smooth skin for the first time in years. It was like touching someone else's flesh; someone who deserved to be clean-shaven; someone better than the man I was.

Anna removed my cape and let the remnants of hair fall to the floor before cleaning up the piles surrounding the chair. I pressed the door closed behind me as I walked into the small bathroom. The reflection of the man in the mirror couldn't have been me. He was pale and clean and human. He stared at me as if questioning why I'd imprisoned him for so long. I felt the need to apologize to him, but the list of sins I'd committed against him was too long to cover in one mea culpa...perhaps even too long to acknowledge in one lifetime.

I let my robe fall to the floor and moved to the shower. Ten minutes later, I was clean, and the bandages on my chest and stomach lay on the shower drain like jellyfish washed ashore on a fiberglass beach. I noticed a pair of flannel pajama pants and a University of Tennessee T-shirt folded neatly on the edge of the sink.

The clean clothes felt almost as alien as the air on my face and head. I'd spent so many years beneath the hair, I'd forgotten how it felt to be me.

Anna sat on the edge of my bed, looking up at me, perhaps admiring her work. "Look at you, professor! I knew you were under there someplace. Look out, George Clooney."

"I'm sorry you had to see me like...you know, before you cut my hair. I didn't realize how much of a difference you would make."

She forced a smile as if she were trying to hold back tears, but there was no reason for her to cry. "You're not what I imagined you'd be. Somehow, I think you might be better than I imagined."

"Do you have it with you?" I asked.

"Have what with me?"

"Your manuscript, of course."

The delight in her voice made me glad I hadn't crushed her dream with my disgruntled view of reality by trying to convince her she was wasting her time trying to unveil universal truths on humanity. Truths are unpalatable for most of humanity, but no purpose would have been served by my cruelty, regardless of its undeniable honesty.

"Yes, I always have it with me. It's on my laptop. I'll email it to you."

I looked down at the bright-eyed innocence of the woman who was, in some ways, still a child. "Do you really think I have an email address?"

Horror filled her eyes. "I'm so sorry. I didn't—"

I laughed, and it hurt, but I couldn't stop. Anna's view of the world assumed everyone's life was full of at least the same luxury, opportunity, and hope as hers. That's probably a commonly held view among most twenty-something college kids. Growing out of that fantasy world is something everyone who lives long enough has to endure. Sometimes it breaks a person, but other times, growing from that stage of blissful ignorance into harsh reality opens a person's eyes to even grander possibilities. They are grounded in recognition and acceptance of the hurdles and pitfalls standing in the way, but strengthened and tempered by the wisdom of experience.

When she realized I wasn't hurt by the innocent email comment, she burst into girlish laughter. Laughing with Anna felt better than anything I could remember.

CHAPTER 10
Am I Crazy?

Anna stood by the window as a gloved nurse replaced the bandages I'd washed from my chest and stomach. "You really shouldn't do that."

"Do what?" I asked.

"Shower without letting someone know."

"I wanted a shower. Anna just cut my hair."

"Yes, I know, and you really shouldn't have let her do that, either. This is a hospital, not a barbershop."

Anna caught my attention and mouthed, "Sorry."

I turned back to the nurse. "Okay, I promise not to do it again. How's that?"

She chuckled. "Somehow, Mr. Millhouse, I don't think you mean that, but you do look nice without that wooly Grizzly Adams beard."

I looked down across my chest as the nurse finished the final bandage. "Thank you, and I do promise to let you know before I shower again."

"I'm not worried about it. Besides, you're not going to be my problem much longer. Your chart says you're leaving us."

Anna turned abruptly from the window. "Leaving? When? Where are you going to go?"

I wasn't looking forward to telling Anna where I was going. My relocation to the psych ward wasn't something I looked forward to telling Anna. I didn't want her to know the doctors thought I was crazy.

Why do I care what she thinks? She's some silly college kid who'll be gone in a few days.

I'd long since stopped caring about other people's opinions of me, but something about Anna made her different.

"They're just moving me upstairs to a different room. That's all."

"Why?"

"I don't know," I lied. "It's just what they do."

Before she could continue her inquisition, Dr. Bernstein came shuffling in. "Whoa! What happened to you?"

I motioned toward Anna. "She gave me a...what did you call it?"

"A transformation."

"That's it. A transformation."

"Well, it worked," said the doctor. "I now understand why you were so excited to see her before moving upstairs."

Anna snapped around, locking her eyes on mine as a huge smile came across her lips. "You were excited to see me?"

I tilted my head innocently. "You said you were coming back, and like you said, it would've been rude if I wasn't here."

My answer appeared to please her, but I didn't understand why that was important to me.

Dr. Bernstein patted his chart. "Well, are we ready to go?"

"Why are you moving him?" Anna asked. "What's wrong with this room?"

The doctor looked questioningly back and forth between Anna and me. "Is she your...."

Unsure of what else to say, I asked, "Could you maybe give us a minute?"

Bernstein nodded in understanding. "Of course. I'll have the nurse help you upstairs in thirty minutes. You look good, John. I think having

Anna around is good for you, and I think you should let her know what's going on."

He patted my shoulder, made a few notes in my chart, and left us alone.

"So, what *is* going on, really?"

I swallowed the pride I'd forgotten I had. "They're moving me upstairs to the seventh floor."

"Yeah, so?"

Clearly, she didn't know what that meant.

"There are things wrong with me that have nothing to do with my wounds, and the specialists for those things are up on the seventh floor."

"What kind of specialists? What aren't you telling me?"

I inhaled a long, painful breath, and then let it out without gasping in pain. "It's the psych ward."

Her face went blank. "Oh."

"Yeah, oh," I replied. "Not exactly like saying I was headed to the podiatrist, is it?"

She sat on the edge of my bed and laid her hand gently on my arm. "You've been through a lot. I'm sure they want to make sure you're okay before they let you go home."

Before the word *home* had fully left her lips, it was obvious she wanted to retract it.

I let her off the hook. "Why are you here, Anna? Finding an author to read your book isn't that hard. You didn't have to go to the trouble of coming here and cutting my hair. What's this all about?"

She cast her eyes toward the floor. "I don't know. Maybe sometimes I think I should be on the seventh floor, too. Ever since I read your first book, I felt like I knew you. And you're not *just* any author. You're a *New York Times* Best-Selling author, and now you're a national hero after what you did in the bookstore."

"So, you're not disappointed that I'm going to the loony bin?"

She frowned. "Don't call it that. That's not nice. And no, I'm not disappointed. I understand, but I want to make sure they'll let me come visit you up there."

"I'm sure they will, and if they don't, I'll sneak out, and we'll smoke cigarettes in the stairwell."

She held up her palm, offering a high five. "It's a date!"

I slapped her palm. "It's a date. Except there's just one problem. I don't smoke."

"Neither do I," she admitted. "But we could eat M&Ms."

"Peanut or plain?"

She grinned. "There's only one kind. Plain."

"Do you have any idea how long it's been since I've had an M&M?"

"We'll see what we can do about ending that streak of bad luck."

Using the pad and pen on the bedside table, she wrote down her cell phone number and handed me the paper. "When they get you upstairs, call me and give me your room number so I can bring you my manuscript tomorrow. I'll print it out and bring you a hard copy since you're all anti-email and stuff."

She shouldered her bag and headed for the door.

"Hey," I called out, and she turned and looked back. "Thanks for the transformation."

She curtsied. "Thanks for letting me do it. See ya tomorrow."

"Bye."

The nurse must've been waiting outside the door. She arrived with an empty wheelchair seconds after Anna left. "All right, Mr. Millhouse, let's get you upstairs."

I looked at the wheelchair and back at the nurse. "There's nothing wrong with my legs. I'd rather walk."

She shrugged. "Sorry, it's hospital policy. If you fall down and get hurt, the hospital's afraid you'll sue them, so you're stuck with me pushing you this time."

I surrendered and stood from my bed, tucking Anna's number into the pocket of the pajama pants she'd brought.

When the elevator doors opened onto the seventh floor, I was surprised to see the space looked just like the other hospital levels. There was no glowing neon sign that read "Loony Bin" flashing on the wall. There were no psychopaths running up and down the halls, setting their hair on fire, and screaming profanity at the top of their lungs.

"This isn't what I expected."

"It never is. Most of the patients up here are a lot like you. They just need a little help and encouragement. Come to think of it, I guess we could all use a little of that now and then."

My room was a mirror image of my previous one downstairs, with two beds, but this time, I was awarded the window seat.

I motioned toward the unmade bed by the door. "Whose is that?"

"I don't know. This isn't my ward. My job is to get you up here and settled in, but I can find out if you want."

"That's not necessary. I was just curious. If I'm going to be in a room with another crazy guy, I want to make sure I'm the crazier of the two."

She tried not to laugh, but her expression told me she felt the same.

I climbed from the wheelchair and sat in the ugly chair by the window. "What time are visitors allowed?"

"I don't know, but you'll meet the nurses soon, and I'm sure one of the doctors will be in to see you."

As nurses tend to be, she was correct. People came in droves: nurses, a psychiatrist, another flock of medical students, and even a dietician. All of them seemed unnecessary to me, except the psychiatrist. I'd known exactly one other psychiatrist in my life: Dr. Murphey from the VA. He was what I assumed all shrinks were like, but I was wrong.

Dr. Michael Oliver was a soft-spoken man who listened with purpose. In my experience, most people don't listen; they merely wait for their turn to talk. Dr. Oliver asked questions—in the form of a question —and then listened as if what I had to say was meaningful.

"How long have you been off the medication, Mr. Millhouse?"

"I don't remember," I admitted, "but it's been several years. When I started drinking, I didn't think I needed it anymore, and then when the whole world came crashing down around me. I didn't have any way to get back to the VA hospital, and at that point, I didn't honestly think about the medication."

"I understand. And you said the psychiatrist's name at the VA was Dr. Murphey. Is that right?"

I imagined Dr. Murphey with his glasses perched on his hawksbill nose and his yellow legal pad poised at the ready. "Yeah, that's right. It was Murphey, but that was twenty years ago, so I doubt if he's still around."

Dr. Oliver made a note in a small spiral-bound notepad. "I'm sure we can find him. I'd like to have your permission to request your medical records from the Army and the VA. Is that all right with you?"

I bit my bottom lip. "Dr. Murphey told me he'd never divulge what we talked about to anyone. I was pretty messed up back then, and I said some stuff that isn't true anymore. I wouldn't want you getting the idea that I'm still that twenty-six-year-old kid from way back then."

The doctor waited several beats before speaking again, presumably to make sure I was finished. He was the best listener I'd ever met. "That's precisely why I'm asking for your permission. I need to know the names of the medication you were on back then, but there's no requirement for you to allow me to see Dr. Murphey's session notes if that makes you uncomfortable."

"I don't remember the names of the meds."

He nodded. "I know, but they'll be in your records. It's likely we've developed new medication since then that's more effective and has fewer side effects. If we can get you on medication that will stabilize your mood and allow you to focus and think clearly, I believe we can make some real strides to getting you back on your feet. How does that sound?"

I stared at him for a long time, but he never looked away. Mine wasn't a challenging stare; it was a hesitation while I tried to decide if I could trust him. His was an attentive, patient state of waiting.

"So, do you *want* to see Dr. Murphey's notes? Do you think they'll be of any value all these years later?"

"What I want doesn't matter, Mr. Millhouse. I'm not in charge. This is your mental health we're talking about, and I would never presume to make demands. It is likely Dr. Murphey's session notes will give me an insight into the events that led you to your current state. If you'd prefer to keep those private, between you and Dr. Murphey, I'll respect that. To get to the bottom of what's causing you to struggle, we can spend as much time together as necessary. It's up to you."

Every time Dr. Oliver opened his mouth, I liked him more. I wasn't a homeless bum to him. In his eyes, I was a patient who was "struggling," as he put it, and he sincerely wanted to help me.

"You can have the notes. I'll sign whatever you need, but I need something from you."

He raised his eyebrows. "Ah, quid pro quo, is it, Mr. Millhouse?"

"No, nothing like that. I just want to know when visiting hours are."

He adjusted his tie. "Well, that's not an easy question to answer. Here in this ward, visitors aren't always the best thing for the recovery of our patients. Sometimes they're more upsetting than soothing, so we have to be very careful about how we handle that. I didn't see any family listed in your chart. Are you expecting someone?"

"She's not my family," I said, "but she is special."

For the first time, Dr. Oliver responded quickly. "Is she a girlfriend or something like that?"

I chuckled. "No, nothing like that. She's an English major, and she wants me to read her manuscript. I told her I would, and I want to keep my word to her."

He made another note in his pad and looked up. "I don't see why that would be a problem. It's kind of you to look over her manuscript. Was she your student?"

I thought about his question. "No, but I think I might be hers."

He smiled. "I'll make sure the nurses know to let her in anytime she comes by. What's her name?"

"Anna."

He waited patiently for a last name, but I didn't have one to offer him.

"Just Anna?" he asked.

"Yes, just Anna."

"Okay, then. There's only one other issue you and I need to discuss this evening. Are you aware that we've been keeping the reporters and journalists at bay?"

"I don't know what you're talking about."

"After what happened in the bookstore, there have been dozens of requests from local and national television and newspaper reporters wanting to interview you."

I looked out the window to make sure there wasn't a group of reporters waiting below. "Why?"

"You're a hero, Mr. Millhouse, and the world is aching for a little good news for a change. Everybody wants an exclusive." He paused and again adjusted his tie. "I'd like to spend a couple of hours with you in session tomorrow before we decide to let the reporters in. Is that okay with you?"

I held up my palms. "Sure. Whatever you say. I don't know why they want to talk to me anyway."

"Good," he said. "That's everything for now. We'll see each other again tomorrow, probably in the early afternoon. Are you having trouble sleeping? I'll be glad to order something to help you rest. Sleep is the closest thing to magic there is."

"That's what Dr. Murphey used to say."

He laughed. "That Dr. Murphey sounds like a smart guy."

"How about if you order the sleeping meds, but don't give them to me unless I can't go to sleep. I'd rather not take anything that isn't necessary."

"Too easy, Mr. Millhouse. Consider it done. Is there anything else?"

"Yeah, just one more thing." I looked past him. "Do you think I'm crazy?"

He slipped his pen into his pocket and leaned in. "Have you ever read *Alice in Wonderland*?"

"Of course I have."

He leaned in even closer and whispered, "All the best people are."

CHAPTER 11
What's in a Name?

Breakfast came at 7:35. It wasn't the same breakfast guy who'd delivered to my previous room. On the seventh floor, breakfast—and I assumed all meals—were delivered by a pair of young women.

When my plate was placed on the table by my bed, I leaned toward the young lady. "I'm really hungry this morning, and I missed dinner last night because they were moving me up here. Do you think there's a chance I could get two plates?"

She smiled knowingly. "Let me see what I can do, sugar. We can probably work something out."

I looked around in a conspiratorial survey of the room and whispered, "Thank you."

A few minutes later, she came back with a second tray and an extra bagel. "Shh. Don't you tell nobody I did this. I need this job."

"It'll be our little secret, I promise. Besides, no one would believe me anyway. I'm crazy."

She giggled. "Crazy like a fox, I'd say. Enjoy your two breakfasts, sugar."

At 7:50, my real reason for requesting the second breakfast came dancing through my door.

"Good morning, professor. The nurses were super cool about letting me come in here. What did you tell them?"

"Good morning, Anna. It's good to see you. I just told them you were someone special, and that it would be nice if they'd let you come in."

"Well, it worked." She manipulated the zipper on her backpack and pulled out a sheaf of paper bound together by an enormous metal clip. "I brought you something."

I slid her breakfast plate toward her and reached for the manuscript.

"Is this for me?" She sheepishly lifted the lid.

"It is. And is this for me?"

"It is," she said with pride. "Oh, and there's something else, too."

She rifled through the pack until she produced a blue and white, four-color pen, and stuck it toward me. "I thought you could maybe mark it up. That pen writes in black, blue, green, and most importantly, red." She pointed toward the butt of the pen. "All you have to do is push down on the color you want from these slidey things right here."

I snatched the pen from her hand, shaking my head. "Yeah, I may be old, but these pens are older than me. I know how it works."

"Thanks for the breakfast," she said.

"You're welcome, but it's not like I bought it. I just asked the lady who brought mine, and I think she liked playing the role of co-conspirator."

"What would you have done with it if I hadn't shown up?"

I reached across, snatched one of her link sausages, and crammed it in my mouth. "I would've eaten it. Trust me. I don't let food go to waste."

As we ate, I leafed through the first chapter of her manuscript. Every time I'd stop running my finger down the paragraphs, she'd lean forward and nervously stare at the page.

"Relax. It's good. Just because I stop moving my finger doesn't mean I've found a mistake. Sometimes I'm pausing to think about what I just read."

"I know, but it's hard to watch someone read your work and not be nervous. Especially somebody like you. You're kind of a big deal."

I almost choked on my eggs. "I'm no deal at all, let alone a big one. I'm afraid you have an overblown idea of who I am. Speaking of that, you don't have to call me professor or Mr. Millhouse. It's okay to call me John or Cap."

She tilted her head and looked into my eyes as if trying to decide if she should tell me a secret or ask me for the car keys. "You are a big deal. You've let yourself forget that. Or maybe you never believed it at all. I don't know. But you're a big deal to me. Of course I knew your real first name was John, but you wrote your books under the name Cap. Why did you do that?"

I would've given her the car keys if I had a car...or a key. "When I first started writing a million years ago, there was a poet named John Millhouse, and he was making a name for himself in the literary world. He published a few books of poetry and even a couple of novels. I didn't want people to get my work confused with his because I was no poet and his novels were nothing like mine, so I published as Cap instead of John."

"I get that." She chewed a bite of a bagel. "But where did you come up with Cap?"

"I was in the Army a lifetime ago, and a lot of people called me Cap, short for Captain. I liked the sound of it, so I stuck with it."

The fact that I was in the Army didn't seem to surprise her. I guessed she'd read it on the dustjacket of my books.

She swallowed the bagel and a mouthful of coffee. "Why'd you get out?"

"Get out of what?"

"The Army, silly."

I didn't like where our conversation was headed, but I had to tell her something. "Ah, my time was up, and I wanted to go back to school."

She looked into my eyes, and I knew she was searching for indications of untruthfulness. I suspect she probably found some. Thankfully, she let me off the hook.

"Okay, well, I have to get to class, but I like having breakfast with you. Maybe we can make it a regular thing, you know, like even when you get out of here."

"Like when I get out of here," I echoed.

"Yeah, exactly. Bye, Professor Cap...or whatever."

The same ladies who delivered the plates came to collect them, and I earned a disapproving glance, followed by a playful wink. "Was that your daughter who just ran outta here with scraps of *your* second breakfast on her shirt?"

Feigning innocence, I smirked, "Why, I wouldn't have any idea who or what you're talking about."

"I'm gonna be keepin' an eye on you, and that's for sure." My co-conspirator leaned in and whispered, "Did you like it?"

"I sure did."

"Good. You let me know when she's comin' back."

* * *

Anna's manuscript consumed me until Dr. Oliver showed up.

"How are you feeling this morning, Mr. Millhouse?"

I held up one finger, motioning for him to wait until I finished the paragraph, then I carefully set the manuscript aside.

"I'm doing okay."

"Good," he said. "What's that you're reading?"

I glanced at the manuscript, deciding how to tell him about Anna. Maybe the truth would do, but in my experience, it rarely sufficed.

"It's Anna's manuscript."

He glanced at the stack of papers and back at me. "Ah, Anna, the English student."

"Yep, that's the one. It's pretty good."

He intentionally repositioned himself between the clock on the wall and me. "What time would you guess it to be?"

I instinctually looked up toward the clock and realized what he'd done. "I guess it's around nine or so."

He smiled and stepped aside, revealing the clock. Ten forty-five.

I shrugged. "I told you it's good."

"It must be good to have held your attention for over two hours. Is it fiction?"

I nodded.

"Tell me about the main character."

"It's a story about—"

"Don't tell me about the story. Tell me about the main character."

"Oh, okay. Well, her name is Caroline, and she's a—"

He interrupted again. "How old is she?"

"Twenty-four."

"Where does she live?"

"Grimes, Tennessee."

"What color is her hair?"

"Well, it doesn't say, but I think it's probably dark brown."

He didn't slow down. "What does she want?"

"She wants to be anywhere other than Grimes, Tennessee."

"Is she in love?"

"No."

"Does she want to be in love?"

"No, I don't think so. I think she just wants to go."

"Is she running from something?"

I had to think about that one. "Yeah, I think she is. I think she's running from her future."

That got his attention.

"Running from her future? What does that mean?"

I sat up. "I think that's what she's doing. She's running from what she's afraid she'll become if she doesn't leave Grimes. She sees most of her friends married to local boys and raising kids. To her, they all seem happy with a simple life in the same place they were born. At first, she envied them, but then she slowly began to question why she didn't want the same things everyone around her seemed to find so much happiness in. Something inside her, like a gypsy spirit, made her want more. It made her curious about what else was out there beyond the county line —beyond every line. The world is tugging at her soul, and Grimes, Tennessee is never going to be able to hold her down."

He was listening intently, just as he'd done the night before, but this time he was doing more than merely listening. He was evaluating and learning. "How's the writing?"

Lying to him would accomplish nothing.

"It's okay. Young, but okay. She has a lot to learn, and there's some awkward dialogue, but for a first effort, especially for a twenty-year-old, it's pretty good."

"Could you have written the story?"

I didn't hesitate. "No. Definitely not. I don't have the frame of reference. I've never been a twenty-four-year-old girl from a small town in Tennessee. I couldn't create a believable character without a frame of reference."

"Where's Anna from?"

That question caught me off guard, and I had to replay the conversations we'd had. "I don't know. I assume she's from here. Somewhere around Knoxville."

"Hmm. I see. So, you've not talked about where she's from."

Is that a question?

I suddenly feared Dr. Oliver was going to turn into the same kind of shrink as Dr. Murphey, asking questions that don't end with a question mark.

As if our session had reached a turning point, Dr. Oliver opened a file folder and fingered through several pages. "I requested your records from the Army and from the VA. We've not heard back from the Army yet, but the VA sent over their records from the time they started treating you in 1993."

I was still waiting for a question.

He continued, listing the medications we'd tried, and finally, the combination that seemed to be most effective back then. "Do you remember those drugs?"

"Well..." I ran my hand over my chin, momentarily shocked to feel bare skin. "Some of the names sound vaguely familiar, but I can't say I remember any of them. That was a long time ago, and a lot has happened since then."

He penciled a note inside the folder. "That's perfectly fine. I wouldn't expect you to remember specifics from almost twenty years ago. Sometimes I can't remember what I had for breakfast."

He continued flipping through the pages and chewing on the eraser end of his pencil. "How did you sleep last night?" He closed the folder and looked directly at me.

"I slept well, and I didn't need the meds you prescribed."

He sighed. "Ah, that's good...very good. If you're okay with it, I'd like to spend an hour together this afternoon. I need to get to know you before we start throwing drugs at a problem that may not be a problem. How do you feel about that?"

"Sure. It's not like I really have a choice, is it?"

He furrowed his brow. "You're not a prisoner here, Mr. Millhouse. Your physical injuries are not severe enough to keep you here, and I've seen nothing that indicates you're an acute danger to yourself or anyone else, so if you don't want my help, or if you feel you don't need my help, I can't keep you here."

"So...I can leave if I want?"

"Well, technically, we need to have the cardiothoracic surgeon and the hospitalist discharge you, but as I said, you're not a prisoner here."

"But if I want to stay and see if maybe you can help me, I can?"

"Yes, of course. Within reason. You can't stay indefinitely, but as long as I feel you will benefit from psychiatric care, we can continue to treat you. Ultimately, your care will need to continue with the VA, but for now, I'm your doctor."

"Does that mean I'll go back to Dr. Murphey when I leave here?"

He opened the file again and flipped to the back. "No, it appears Dr. Murphey doesn't work for the VA any longer, but I would like to talk with him. If he's still practicing, would you also like to talk with him?"

"I don't know," I said. "I doubt he's very happy with me since I stopped taking the meds and ended up like this."

Dr. Oliver smiled. "I don't know, Dr. Murphey, but if you were my patient and I hadn't seen you in twenty years, I'd definitely want to see you again."

I almost laughed. "Yeah, but I don't think you and Dr. Murphey have much in common other than both of you being shrinks. He has a much different approach to treatment than you do."

"Maybe," he said, "but for the most part, doctors want to see their patients doing well, and psychiatrists—or shrinks, as you like to call us—are no different. So, I'll see you around two p.m. this afternoon, okay?"

"Sure."

"Okay, then. Two o'clock." He tapped the edge of my bed with the folder. "Oh, one more thing...."

"Yeah, what is it?"

"What's Anna's last name?"

A feeling of embarrassment came over me for not knowing, but I reached for the manuscript and flipped to the title page: *Anywhere but Here by Anna Hollenbeck.*

When I read her last name, my heart stopped.

"Mr. Millhouse, are you all right?"

His words echoed in my head as if they were tumbling down a bottomless well, and the world around me began to melt into dripping streams of reality, dissolving into emptiness. My breath came in shallow, gasping jerks, and the inside of my mouth turned to sand. I couldn't comprehend what I'd just learned, and a chill consumed me to my core.

"Mr. Millhouse, what's going on? Talk to me."

I could hear him calling my name, but it was as if I were in a coma and couldn't respond. The doctor took my arm in his hand, and I lashed out, striking at his wrist and knocking his hand away. My breath was coming in painful gasps, and everything went out of focus. I threw the manuscript across the room and watched the pages separate, falling like leaves to the ground.

Leaping from my bed, I flipped the table from its casters and sent it flying toward the window. Dr. Oliver stepped between me and the door, but I plowed through him as if he weren't there. When I made it through the doorway and into the hall, I couldn't remember which way I'd come in. I didn't know how to get out. I was trapped, and the inside of my head was ringing. The floor wavered like pudding, and I stumbled, grabbing at anything, but I couldn't find purchase. I was collapsing. Imploding.

The last thing I remember before the world turned dark was two pairs of strong hands clamping on to me and a needle penetrating my left arm.

CHAPTER 12
Freedom's Vow

When I came to, I had no idea where I was or why I was tied to the bed. Leather bindings held me in place, and an IV line was attached to my left arm. I lay in silence, trying to remember what put me in that position.

What did I do? What's happening to me?

The room was dim but not completely dark. A heart monitor shone a yellow glow and sang a monotonous beat while a single lamp in the corner of the room glowed a faint essence that seemed otherworldly from my prison bed. I was thirsty and hungry and confused.

A beam of harsh fluorescent light penetrated the room as the door swung inward and Dr. Oliver's silhouette appeared in the opening. He stood a safe distance away from me and looked down on his bound patient. "How are you feeling, Mr. Millhouse?"

"Confused," I admitted, holding up my wrists and displaying my confinement. "What's this all about?"

He spoke in a soft, measured monotone. "Do you remember what happened, Mr. Millhouse?"

"No, I have no idea, but it must've been pretty bad if this is the result."

"You became extremely agitated after discovering Anna's last name on the cover of her manuscript, and you reacted somewhat aggressively. We were forced to sedate you for your own protection and for the protection of the hospital staff. We had no other choice."

Parts of the scene Dr. Oliver described flashed through my mind, and I wanted to cry.

What have I done? Why didn't Anna tell me the truth about who she is? How long have I been sedated?

"What time is it?" I asked.

He checked his watch. "It's just before nine."

"Nine? At night?"

Dr. Oliver placed his hand on the foot of my bed. "No, Mr. Millhouse. It's nine a.m. on Wednesday morning."

"Wednesday?" I said in disbelief. "But I thought it was Monday."

As if things like that were routine in the loony bin, he said, "It was Monday when you experienced the reaction. We've kept you sedated until this morning. You were extremely agitated when we allowed you to wake up yesterday, so I administered some medication to help you relax and let your mind come to terms with the situation."

"I'm really sorry. I didn't mean to.... I didn't hurt anyone, did I?"

"No, you didn't hurt anyone, but based on your condition, I believed you might have hurt yourself or someone else. That was the reason we had to sedate you."

"Has Anna seen me like this?"

"No. Only the hospital staff."

The tears came, but my bindings prevented me from wiping them away. I turned my head to dry my face on the pillow. "I don't want her to see me like this."

The doctor pursed his lips. "I think it's best if you don't see Anna at all for a while. I fear you may have a negative reaction to her presence. We need to work on—"

"No!" I demanded. "I have to see her. I have to see her now!"

"Mr. Millhouse, I need you to relax. It's not possible to see Anna right now. In time, when we've resolved some of these issues, we'll consider letting you see her again, but for now, that simply is not an option."

The tears still came, at first driven by embarrassment, but they soon became cries of empty sadness. I wanted to see Anna. I needed to know the truth.

"Are you hungry, Mr. Millhouse?"

I nodded, willing the tears to stop, but to no avail. They continued their onslaught until I finally surrendered and let them come.

A nurse came in and fed me Jell-O with a plastic spoon, making me feel like a helpless infant confined to a highchair.

"I won't let it happen again. Please take the restraints off of my wrists."

She suppressed the compassion in her eyes. "I'm sorry, Mr. Millhouse. It's not up to me. I can't do that, but if you'll remain calm and relaxed, I'm sure Dr. Oliver will remove them very soon. Okay?"

It wasn't okay, but it didn't matter. I was now his prisoner instead of his patient. Earning my freedom and his trust would be agonizing, but I had no other choice. Being reduced to a caged animal incapable of feeding himself left me wishing I'd never awakened from the sedation.

What difference would it make to the world if one less lunatic didn't wake up? It would be a cleaner, safer, and saner place.

Those thoughts weren't new to me, but the next one certainly was.

I can't die. I have to know the truth about Anna and why she hid the truth from me.

Dr. Oliver returned and stood closer to my bed but still slightly beyond my reach. He spoke in his typical calming tone. "We started medication through your IV that should help prevent another outburst like you had on Monday. It's a combination of drugs similar to the ones Dr. Murphey prescribed twenty years ago. The difference is that these particular drugs are believed to work in a different part of the brain, allowing you to think clearly but avoid unwanted physical reactions to stress."

He paused as if he wanted me to say something, but I had nothing. I didn't have any choice which drugs they pumped into my veins, so I was relegated, at least in my mind, to their guinea pig.

"Now that you're fully awake and you've had something to eat, how are you feeling?"

"Physically?"

"Sure, we'll start with how you're feeling physically. Tell me about that."

I rattled my restraints. "These are uncomfortable. My back hurts from being in this bed for three days. I'm dirty, and I want a shower."

"All of those things are perfectly reasonable. How about psychologically?"

"I'm ashamed and embarrassed."

A smile wasn't what I expected. I was the crazy one, but his reaction didn't seem appropriate.

"That's normal. Shame and embarrassment are the feelings I hoped you'd have."

"You hoped I'd feel like this?" I asked.

"My hope is we'll find a combination of medications that keeps you stable enough to deal with things that would otherwise send you into another episode such as Monday's, but these are excellent indications that you're experiencing normal human emotion."

I didn't know if that was supposed to make me feel better or worse, but regardless of the intent, I certainly didn't feel any better.

"Would you like for me to remove the restraints?" he asked abruptly.

I stared down at my bound hands. "Yes, I'd like that."

"I'll remove them, but it's crucial you remain calm. If you demonstrate any attempts to harm yourself or anyone else, I'll have no choice but to put the restraints back in place immediately. Do you understand?"

The overwhelming need to apologize consumed me, but I couldn't create the words without tearing up, so I blinked and nodded.

He took a step toward my bed. "Okay, John. I'll be right back."

When he returned, he wasn't alone. A nurse who looked like he'd been a college linebacker stood to the doctor's left, and another stood to his right. The much smaller and less threatening of the two held a syringe in her hand and wore a look of cautious optimism.

Dr. Oliver put his hand on my arm. "Are you going to remain calm, John?"

I nodded again, but that wasn't good enough.

"I need you to answer me before I can remove the restraints. Are you going to remain calm?"

"I am. I promise."

He unbuckled the heavy leather strap and let my hand slide free. I expected him to leap backward in fear for his life, but he stood by my side and let the restraint fall beside the bed with one end still firmly attached to the frame. The freedom I felt after having only one arm unlashed was overwhelming. It felt as if I'd been pulled from the water after nearly drowning.

"Thank you," I whispered.

He smiled, but this time it wasn't associated with my healthy psychological response. It was a sincere smile that said, "You're welcome."

I lifted my right hand, offering it to him.

"No," he said, "I have to remove that one from the other side."

Leaning across a dangerous crazy man was obviously against protocol, and that made sense. He rounded the foot of my bed, relaxed and unconcerned. If I were going to hurt him, that would have been the perfect time, but I had no desire to harm him or anyone else.

He disconnected the restraint from my right wrist and then both of my ankles. The relief was astonishing. I wouldn't do anything ever again to deserve that treatment. Confinement is beyond the limit at which I can consider myself human. If I have to be chained up like a wild animal, I'm not suitable for living. I silently vowed I would do anything to remain human and free.

CHAPTER 13
Honorable Men

I rubbed at my wrists as the two nurses relaxed. The linebacker even smiled.

I returned his gaze. "I'm glad you weren't necessary."

The big man cracked his knuckles. "Yeah, me too."

Dr. Oliver took the syringe from the second nurse and slid it into his lab coat pocket. "There. Is that better?"

"Thank you. I'm sorry for all the trouble I caused. I won't let it happen again."

He pulled the chart from the foot of my bed and made a note, probably logging the time my restraints came off. I hoped that would be the last mention of the restraints.

"Would you like to take a shower?"

That wasn't the question I thought was coming, but there was only one answer. "Absolutely."

"I'll have the nurse come back and remove your bandages. There's no shower in this room, so they'll show you where it is."

I should've known it would be the linebacker who Dr. Oliver would send.

"Let me guess. They didn't hire you because you were the nurse with the best bedside manner."

He almost laughed. "Well, not exactly."

It didn't take him long to have the bandages removed from my torso. When I tried to stand, the time I'd spent confined in the bed became evident; I felt as though I was crawling from a tiny box. My knees trembled in protest of supporting my weight, and long burning aches tore through my back.

When I took my first step, my body didn't cooperate, and the linebacker nurse caught me before I collapsed. I didn't resist primarily because I was thankful for being caught, but also because I didn't want him thinking I was interested in mixing it up with him. I'd lose and end up back in leather handcuffs.

He helped me regain my balance. "Are you okay?"

"I think so, but I'm a little woozy."

"*Woozy* is a good word for it," he said. "The medication you're on sometimes has that effect. I'll make sure Dr. Oliver knows, and he'll get you on the correct dosage. It may take a few days, though."

"I understand," I said, trying not to look like Bambi on ice.

After a few strides towards the bathroom, my legs joined the effort, and walking became less demanding.

"Everything you need is on the sink," he said. "Do you want me to stay with you?"

"I think I'll be okay," I said, "but don't go far."

"You got it, Mr. Millhouse. I'll be around. Let me know when you're ready to go back to your room."

The shower felt like a little dose of heaven. I let the hot water run across my face and shoulders, washing away the previous three days. I'd been given shaving cream and a safety razor, so I did my best to recreate the results Anna accomplished on Monday. Bathing and shaving were luxuries I'd long forgotten. The simplest of things are sometimes the most important, and are often the things we take most for granted.

I wiped the fog from the mirror and looked at the old man staring back at me. He'd aged since Monday, but he looked better than he had for most of a decade.

The linebacker returned. "I'll take you back to your room. Do you want to go back to the one you were in on Monday, or would you prefer another?"

"What's your name?" I asked the big man.

"Phillip."

"Okay, Phillip. I'd love to go back to my old room."

He grinned. "Okay, then. Away we go. Would you like to walk or ride?"

"Are we talking wheelchair or piggyback?"

He laughed. "If I gave you a piggyback ride, they'd put *me* in restraints. It'll have to be a wheelchair."

"In that case, I think I'd rather walk."

He returned me to the room where I'd acted like a perfect jackass forty-eight hours earlier. I wanted that room again to prove to the staff —and to myself—that I could behave like a rational human being, even in an environment where I'd behaved like an animal.

Dr. Oliver came in shortly after. "Do you feel like talking about what happened?"

Talking about it was inevitable, but I still didn't like the idea. "Have you read Dr. Murphey's notes from when I came home from Colombia?"

Psychiatrists are different during sessions. They look, behave, and sound different when they transform themselves into counselors.

He pulled up a chair, crossed his legs, and took on his shrink persona. "I have, and I now understand why you were so upset on Monday. I must say I'm curious about Anna's motivations, and I'm sure you are as well."

I stared at the ceiling and thought about the afternoon at Sherry Hollenbeck's home all those years before. I could smell her skin and almost taste her tears. Allowing myself to succumb to her physical expression of grief sickened me. What kind of pervert had I been? Why didn't I console her without letting her lead me into her bedroom? Why had I not been an honorable man like her husband? There could be no consolation or rationalization for my unthinkable actions on that day. If there was one unbreachable obstacle between me and sanity, it was my despicable behavior on that day, and I'd never overcome it.

"That name—Hollenbeck," I said. "It's too unique to be a coincidence. Anna is Payne and Sherry's daughter. She looks like her mother looked twenty years ago. The same dimple and dark hair and eyes. Why would she seek me out?"

He took a long, deep breath. "I don't know, John. Perhaps there's an explanation that isn't sinister in nature. Perhaps it's perfectly innocent."

"Perfectly innocent? How could it be anything other than sinister?"

"I wish I had an answer for you, John, but I don't. I would, however, like to talk with her and try to get to the bottom of this. She's been here several times since Monday asking to see you, but we obviously couldn't allow that."

I tried to imagine how that counseling session would look and feel. The two greatest demons I'd ever face were my regret over sleeping with Sherry Hollenbeck and the torturous memory of me getting her husband killed in the Colombian jungle. Sitting in a room with Sherry, her daughter, and Dr. Oliver terrified me.

I shifted my eyes to his. "What would you ask her?"

"Well, I'd start by asking her about her childhood, then work my way through her education until I could finally explore her motivations to study English and to write a novel. In doing so, I believe I can piece together her reasons for seeking you out and going to such elaborate lengths to ingratiate herself to you."

"What if she lies?"

He lowered his chin and raised an eyebrow. "I've been doing this a long time, John. If she lies, I'll know, and I'll make her understand that lying won't result in any positive outcome. If her intentions are sinister, I'll see that she has no further access to you, and I'll make sure you have the means to legally prevent her from approaching you again."

I stared down at my hands that had once created books referred to as "modern masterpieces"; the hands that had once held the controls of multi-million-dollar helicopters in training, peacetime, and in combat. "What if her motivations are innocent?"

"Well, John, if that's the case, you'll have to decide if you want to see her again. She may hold the key to your recovery, but it's impossible to know without talking to her."

I carefully considered what he said. Maybe she was my helicopter after I'd sent the two boats away. "What if she doesn't want to talk to you?"

"I can't force her to talk with me, but I can certainly encourage her to do so, especially if she truly cares about you. I'm going to let you in on a little secret, John. If her motives are sinister, she won't be able to resist talking to me."

"Do you need my permission to talk to her?"

"No, certainly not. But you're my patient, and I have a responsibility to you. It's my job to do everything in my power to get you back on the road to living a productive, healthy life, and if interviewing Anna Hollenbeck plays a role in that, I absolutely want to make it happen."

"Then I suppose you should talk to her."

"I'll do that, John. Now, let's talk about what happened on Monday."

The knot in my gut hardened at the impending scolding that I knew I deserved, but it didn't make it any easier to swallow. I'd yelled at myself more than enough in the previous two decades; surely I could take one tongue-lashing from Dr. Oliver. I mentally squared my shoulders and prepared for the blow, but it didn't come.

Instead of punching me in the face, he patted me on the back. "John, while reading Dr. Murphey's session notes, I realized that what happened inside your head on Monday is understandable. You've been harboring a mountain of self-hatred over what happened in Ms. Hollenbeck's home all those years ago, but it's time for you to accept that you can never change what happened, and continuing to punish yourself for it is futile."

"That's easy for you to say. You didn't do it. You're not guilty of that atrocity."

"No, John, you're right, I've never experienced anything like that. But twenty years is long enough. You've served your sentence. You owe it to yourself and society to do what is necessary to put it behind you and return to the life you deserve—the life you worked so hard to earn. You're educated far beyond ninety-nine percent of the world. You're a *New York Times* Best-Selling author, and by all accounts, a brilliant English professor. You have a great deal to offer the world. If for no other reason, John, consider your work a penance to yourself and to society. Don't keep that brilliance pent up and hidden. Put it to work for good."

I stared at the doctor. "Is this a therapy session or a pep talk?"

"It's both. I wouldn't be much of a psychiatrist if I didn't listen *and* encourage. You need and deserve both."

This approach to mental health was one I hadn't experienced, and I wondered if my life would've been different if Dr. Oliver had been my psychiatrist at the VA two decades before.

"I have another question, doc. Why did you start calling me John instead of Mr. Millhouse when I woke up this morning?"

He glanced at the floor as if he were deciding how to answer. "I'm going to be perfectly honest with you because that's what I expect from you. Dr. Murphey wrote in his notes that you respond most positively to being called by your first name. You may not think he was the best doctor for your needs back then, but he was at least right about that. You do seem to respond better to John rather than Mr. Millhouse."

"Thank you for the honesty, doc. I appreciate it."

"You don't have to thank me, John. It's quid pro quo. I tell you the truth, and you tell me the truth. That's the only way we'll make any progress."

I could deal with that arrangement. In fact, I wished the whole world could work under those terms.

I held out my hand. To my surprise, he looked me in the eye, and we shook hands like honorable men. I would keep my end of the bargain, and I had every reason to believe he'd do the same.

CHAPTER 14
A Writer

That night, a nurse delivered three pills in a tiny paper cup that looked like it should've contained ketchup from a pump dispenser.

"What are these?" I asked.

"They're the meds Dr. Oliver prescribed. Two are for mood stabilization, and one is to help you sleep. You know what they say. Sleep is the closest thing to magic."

Everyone in the field of psychology must be trained to recite that phrase.

I swallowed the pills, and the nurse made a note in my chart. I can't attest to the effectiveness of the mood stabilizers, but the sleeping pill worked like a charm.

When I awoke the following morning, my favorite breakfast lady was walking through my door. "Welcome back, Mr. Millhouse. I missed you. I'm not supposed to ask, but how are you doing?"

Remembering our conspiracy game, I peered around her in perfect cloak-and-dagger style. "Don't tell anyone, but I'm perfectly sane. I just let them think I'm crazy so you'll keep bringing me breakfast."

She snapped a glance over each shoulder and whispered, "Don't you tell anyone, but I'm as crazy as an outhouse rat. I just keep bringing you breakfast so they'll think I'm sane."

"We've got a good thing going here," I said. "Let's not screw it up."

She made pistols with her thumbs and index fingers and pointed both of them at me. "It's a deal. Two plates this morning?"

I sighed. "No, unfortunately, I made an ass of myself on Monday, so I'm in solitary confinement until I prove I can behave."

"Ah, we all have bad days. I've got faith in you."

She set my plate on the table, removed the lid, and then emptied the contents of the second plate onto the first. With her index finger against her lips, she said, "Shh...don't tell anybody."

"It'll be our little secret, but if we're going to keep up this game, I need to know your name."

She held out her nametag. "I'm Gladys, but you can call me Gladys."

"You really are crazy, aren't you?"

"If you only knew. Oh, the stories I could tell."

I couldn't resist grinning from ear to ear. "Thank you, Gladys. Now get out of here before we get busted for stealing eggs and sausage links. I'm not going back to prison for you."

As she made her way to the exit, she waved her arms in the air. "They'll never take us alive!"

I was beginning to believe I was the only sane one in the whole ward.

After breakfast, I was surprised to see the hospitalist, Dr. Bernstein, shuffling into my room in his typical foot-dragging gait.

"Good morning, Mr. Millhouse. Do you remember me?"

"Of course I remember you, Dr. Bernstein. I may be crazy, but my memory still works."

"Good. Now, let's take a look at those wounds."

I pulled my gown over my chest and stomach, revealing the bandages. One by one, he removed them, carefully examining each wound.

"I think we can leave these open and let them get some fresh air. How are you feeling?"

"I had a rough few days, but I'm getting better. I actually feel pretty good."

He looked concerned. "By rough few days, do you mean you were in pain?"

"No, not physical pain. I just had a little breakdown."

Relief replaced concern. "Oh, good."

I found that to be an odd response, but I found most things about Dr. Bernstein to be odd.

"Okay, then. We'll leave the bandages off, and I'll make an annotation in your chart."

He lifted the clipboard from the foot of my bed, and his eyes widened. "Oh, my. You did have a rough few days."

I held up my hands in the universal I-don't-know sign. "I don't remember most of it."

He made an entry in the chart. "Well, it looks like you're making some wonderful progress. I'll check on you in a couple of days, but in the meantime, if those wounds give you any trouble, tell one of the nurses, and we'll take another look. We'll take the stitches out in a few days."

"Whatever you say. You're the doctor."

"Have a good day, Mr. Millhouse."

He vanished, and I realized I was missing *The Price Is Right*.

Just before lunchtime, Dr. Oliver came in wearing a confident look. "Hello, John. How are you feeling?"

I rattled off the answer he was expecting. "I'm doing okay."

"That's good. I had a talk with Anna this morning, and she wants to see you."

He suddenly had my full attention. "Are you going to let her?"

"That's up to you, John, but first, you need to know what I learned."

I sat up in the bed and focused intently. "Tell me."

He removed his glasses and propped up against the foot of my bed. "I spent an hour with her, and I believe she has no idea you knew her father or her mother."

"How can that be? It's too big to be a coincidence."

He shook his head. "Oh, I agree. It's definitely no coincidence, but it is an interesting collection of events that led her to you. I think you should hear it from her, though. How do you feel about that?"

The thought of seeing Anna again conjured up a plethora of emotions. On the one hand, I wanted to see her. I liked her. But on the other hand, I still questioned her motives and feared she was waiting to spring a trap.

"Will you be there when she comes to see me?"

He cocked his head in obvious interest. "Do you want me to be there?"

"I don't know," I admitted. "Maybe."

"Why would you want me to be there, John?"

I wanted to lie, but I'd shaken the man's hand and agreed to tell him the truth. "I'm afraid I won't be able to tell if she's lying to me."

"That's an honest answer. I'll leave it up to you. If you want me there, I'll sit in. If you don't, I won't. I believe the medication is working nicely, and you'll be able to deal with whatever happens when she comes to visit, but if you're concerned, I'm more than happy to stay in the room."

I stared at the ceiling, my go-to move when I needed to think about what was happening around me. "When?"

"When what, John?"

"When will you let her come see me?"

"I told her she could come back tomorrow afternoon. Is that okay with you?"

"Yes, tomorrow afternoon is a good time. Can I have a shower and a shave before she comes?"

"Of course you can. You don't have to ask to bathe."

"I just want to be presentable when she shows up."

"I understand. She says she doesn't have classes on Friday afternoons, so I told her to be here tomorrow at one o'clock. If that doesn't work for you, I can cancel or reschedule."

"No, no. One o'clock is good. I don't know if I want you to be in here or not, though. Can I have some time to think about that?"

"Take all the time you need. I'll leave my schedule open for tomorrow afternoon. Let me know what you decide."

"Thank you, Dr. Oliver. I know you don't have to go to the lengths you are, but it means a lot to me."

"It's my job, John. It's what I do."

He headed for the door, but I stopped him. "Oh, one more thing."

"Sure, what is it?"

"Do you think there's any way I could get that manuscript back?"

He grinned. "Yeah, I think we can do that."

I spent the day reading the remainder of Anna's manuscript. It didn't take long for me to abandon the professorial approach and begin reading for the pure joy of reading—something I hadn't done in years. Her story was captivating, and it made me temporarily forget my problems and care about Anna's main character. That's the mark of a great writer. If a writer can pull a reader from his world and have him willingly immerse himself into the world created on the pages, then she is truly a writer. Anna Hollenbeck was, most certainly, a writer.

CHAPTER 15
Freakin' Picasso

March 9, 2012

I should've been nervous, but for some reason, I wasn't. Perhaps that was further evidence of my insanity. I read someplace that irrational responses to stimuli are one of the hallmarks of abnormal psychology, but just because I didn't behave or react the way most people would, didn't necessarily mean I belonged in the psych ward.

I showered and shaved, ate lunch, and sat in the ugly brown chair by the window, awaiting Anna's arrival. I had no plan, no outline of what we'd discuss, or any reason to believe she'd have one. I wondered what Dr. Oliver had told her about why she'd been kept away from me for four days, but ultimately, it didn't matter. My sequestration from the outside world would come to an end in less than ten minutes.

When the door swung inward, I was disappointed to see Dr. Oliver alone. He closed the door behind him and sat on the edge of my bed. "Good afternoon, John. How are you?"

"I'm excited," I blurted out.

"That's good." He glanced at the clock on the wall. "Anna will be here soon, so it's time to decide if you want me here during your conversation."

"I've thought about that a lot, doc, and I think I'd like you to be here. At some point, if we decide to talk privately, you'd be okay with that, wouldn't you?"

"Of course I would, John. I'll stay out of the way and just listen. If you want me involved at any point, feel free to invite me into the conversation. Otherwise, I'll be practically invisible."

"One more thing," I said. "What reason did you give Anna for not being able to see me?"

"I told her you had a little accident and couldn't have visitors for a few days, but she's pretty smart, John. I think she knows there's more to it than that. I can't tell you what you can and can't talk about with her, but I'd like to encourage you to be as honest as possible. If you two are going to build a relationship, no matter how brief, lies are only going to serve to weaken that relationship."

I stared out the window, thinking about what a relationship with the daughter of Payne and Sherry Hollenbeck could possibly entail. "Can I ask her why she didn't tell me who she really is?"

"Again, I can't tell you what to say to her, but you might want to save that question for the end. What you learn before asking a question like that might be more meaningful than anything her answer would reveal."

Well, that was cryptic.

I trusted Dr. Oliver, so I'd do my best to take his advice.

He slapped his knees and stood up. "Okay, then. I guess it's time to bring in the guest of honor."

The nervousness I hadn't previously felt suddenly poured over me in waves. *What should I say? What should she say? Will I get angry again? What if she doesn't trust me anymore?*

My paranoia vanished the instant Anna came bursting through the door. She ran to me with her arms outstretched and threw them around my neck in the most sincere hug I'd felt in years. I returned her embrace, and we held each other for a long, precious moment. When she released her grasp on me and leaned back, I saw her mother's face where hers should've been: the dimple, the dark eyes, and the beautiful turned-up nose.

She took my face in her hands. "Look at you, all clean-shaven and looking so handsome...just like George Clooney. I've missed you, professor."

"I've missed you too, Anna. I'm sorry about what happened." I didn't expect to apologize to her, but somehow it seemed like the right thing to do.

She looked bewildered. "Why would you be sorry? Whatever happened, it was an accident."

The skin between my eyes wrinkled in confusion. "No, Anna. It wasn't an accident. When I saw your last name on the cover of your manuscript, it brought back some memories I didn't want to relive, and I reacted poorly...to say the least."

Her expression didn't change. "I don't understand. Why would my name upset you?"

At that moment, we were both confused beyond explanation, and I turned to Dr. Oliver, who was, as he'd promised, sitting silently in the corner of the room. He offered no advice or direction, although I was certain he knew exactly what should be said next.

The question I so badly longed to ask was burning on the tip of my tongue, but I followed the doctor's advice and saved it. Instead of asking why she kept her name from me, I said, "Why did you seek me out, Anna? Why me? And how did you find me?"

"What do you mean, professor? Those are silly questions. I sought you out because my mom loved your books. They were some of the first novels I ever read, all because she loved them so much. You were a household name for me growing up. You're the reason I wanted to come to school at UT. You wrote the creative writing curriculum, and even though you weren't teaching anymore, some of the professors and instructors in the English department learned from you. I've known I wanted to be a writer since the first time I read your first book. Oh, and I found you because of that thing at the bookstore. I saw it on the news."

Nothing was getting clearer. Everything she said only muddied the already-murky waters of my mind. "Your mother read my books?"

She struck a look I couldn't identify. "Duh. Yeah, she read your books."

"Why?"

"This conversation is getting weird. You're like my mom's favorite author. I mean, you're good and all, but she thought you were better than Stephen King and James Patterson. Back then, I didn't know why. She just liked you."

It was becoming clear Anna had no idea who I was. She didn't know I was with her father when he died, and she obviously had no idea what happened between her mother and me.

"Anna," I said, "I think there's something you should know."

I heard Dr. Oliver reposition in his chair, and I looked up to see his eyes as wide as saucers.

"Okay, what do you think I should know?" She seemed quite impatient.

I cleared my throat and gathered my courage. "I met your mother once."

She started nodding. "Oh, yeah, I know. I was there."

"What? You were there?"

"Yeah, I was there. It was at Barnes and Noble in Huntsville. I was eight or nine. We stood in line to get you to sign my mom's books. I thought it was dumb at the time, but when I got older and I read your stuff, I understood, and I thought it was pretty cool."

"You came to a book signing?"

"I sure did, with my mom. That's when you met her, right? How do you remember meeting her? I mean, why her, out of all those people? And you must've done a thousand book signings. It's weird that you'd remember meeting my mom."

Dr. Oliver exhaled the breath he'd been holding, but I still wasn't sure I was going take advantage of Anna letting me off the hook so easily.

"How could I forget anyone dragging a little girl as cute as you all the way to a boring old book signing?"

The doctor smiled, and Anna rolled her eyes. "Yeah, sure, whatever. So, did you read my manuscript?"

The subject changed, and part of me was thankful. The truth is a good thing, but not always the whole truth. I had no memory of signing books in Huntsville and certainly no memory of Sherry Hollenbeck being there.

"Yes, I did read it. In fact, I read it twice."

"Yeah? So? What do you think? It's bad, isn't it?" She slumped in her chair. "I know. Nobody would read it, right?"

Her self-doubt reminded me of how I felt every time I finished a manuscript. Every day I believed I'd wake up with the world having discovered that I was a terrible writer, and my books would instantly stop selling. Self-doubt is the most common characteristic of writers. We all believe our books suck, and we can't believe anyone actually buys them. In my experience, the best writers are the ones who suffer most from those demons of doubt.

"No, Anna. You're wrong. It's good. In fact, it's the best first manuscript I've ever read by any author, and I've read hundreds, if not thousands. Yours is better than good."

She blushed. "You're just saying that. You don't mean it."

"Yes, I do. It wouldn't do any good for me to lie to you. If it sucked and I encouraged you to publish it, when it didn't sell, your heart would break, and my opinion would be meaningless to you forever. I wouldn't do that to you. I mean it. It's really good."

She collapsed backward into the chair. "Oh, my God. Mom's never gonna believe this. Cap Millhouse said my manuscript is good."

Anna leapt to her feet and threw her arms around me again. "This is the best day of my life." She kissed me on the cheek. "So, what do I do now?"

"What do you mean? What do you do about what?"

"My manuscript, silly. What do I do with it now that it's written and you like it?"

The lump in my throat returned at the thought of what I was about to admit. "I'm sorry. I don't know."

"What do you mean you don't know? You're a famous writer, and you were on the *New York Times*—"

"Anna, I've been living on the street and in shelters for over ten years. I've not written a word in over a decade. I have no idea how the publishing business works now."

The sadness in her eyes almost brought tears to mine. "Why?"

The look on her face reminded me of her mother's the day I told her the truth about what happened in the Colombian jungle.

"I don't know exactly why, but that's part of the reason I'm here. Dr. Oliver is trying to help me get back on my feet and work through the problems I have."

She tilted her head in concerned interest. "What problems? You had it all. You were a great professor and a famous writer. What problems could you have possibly had that made you throw all that away?"

Dr. Oliver rose from his chair, obviously preparing to leap to my defense, but I held up my hand. "No. It's okay. She's right, and I'm going to tell her the truth."

He slowly closed his eyes and shook his head in blatant disapproval of my plan.

"Anna, I was in the Army a long time ago, and some bad stuff happened." I held up my battered thumbs, showing her the remnants of the torture I'd endured. "I was with some incredibly brave men who died on a mission. In fact, I was the only one who survived."

"That's terrible," she said. "I'm sorry you had to go through that."

"When I got home, I was pretty messed up, and I ended up going to the VA to get some help for the thoughts I was having. I blamed myself for those men dying. I made a lot of mistakes, and I did a lot of terrible things. Some of those things...one in particular...."

"It was a war," she said. "Terrible stuff happens in wars. I know. My daddy died before I was born. He was in the Army, too. He got killed in South America. My mom was pregnant with me when he died, and he never knew about me. But I've got pictures of him. If you want, I could show them to you sometime."

I locked eyes with the doctor, and he adamantly shook his head, practically ordering me not to tell her.

I followed his unspoken order and returned to my version of the truth. "I'm sorry about your dad, Anna."

"It's okay. Bad stuff happens all the time...like what happened to Kristy and P.J."

"Kristy and P.J? Who are they?"

"They were my brother and sister. P.J, Payne Junior, was named after my dad. He was almost three years older than me. Kristy was a year younger than him. They drowned in a boating accident at summer camp when I was five. You had to be six to go to the camp, so I couldn't go. Otherwise, I would've been in the boat with them. Anyway, after that, it was just Mom and me, and we got really close. We were all each other had, so there was no choice. We had to stick together."

I was frozen in disbelief. Her brother and sister *and* father died horrible deaths, and she was going to school and writing beautifully.

How can she be so strong with all of that loss in her short life? How can I be so weak?

"Anna, I don't know what to say."

She waved a dismissive hand. "You couldn't have known. It's fine. It sucks, but I deal, and I found out writing helps."

I bit my lip to keep from crying. "Yeah, it sure does."

Her eyes widened. "Hey, has it really been ten years since you've written anything?"

"Longer than that," I admitted.

"Will you write something for me?"

My jaw dropped, and I stared at her, wholly unsure what to say.

She saved me. "It's okay. I'm sorry. Never mind. It was a dumb idea anyway."

The words came from deep inside me but weren't created from conscious thought. "No, it's not a dumb idea. I'd love to write something for you. What do you want me to write?"

She rolled her eyes again. "That's like Picasso asking what you want him to paint for you. It doesn't freakin' matter what you write. It's going to be amazing. Mom is going to freak out. She'll never believe me. She's gonna think I'm making it up."

"I don't have anything to write on. I don't even own a pen. Do you think you could get me a composition book...and a pen?"

She looked terrified. "I didn't bring my backpack. I don't have class this afternoon, but I can bring one back later if that's okay."

For the first time, Dr. Oliver spoke. "I think we can find you something to write on...and probably even a pen."

Anna turned to thank him and caught a glimpse of the clock. "Oh, shoot. I've got to run. I'm tutoring at the student center this afternoon."

She hopped to her feet and turned back to me. "Thank you, professor. This has been great. And thank you, too, Dr. Oliver. Can I come back again tomorrow?"

"Yes, Anna," the doctor said. "You may come back whenever you'd like."

She grinned like a little girl. "This has been the best day ever."

"Thank you so much, professor. I can't tell you what all this means to me. Really, I mean it. Thank you."

"Don't thank me, Anna. You're the one who deserves the thanks. I'm amazed and impressed with everything about you. And, hey, you don't have to call me professor. Call me John...or Cap, if you'd like."

When Anna left the room, Dr. Oliver stood. "John, that was amazing. You're changing that girl's life."

"No, doc. That girl's changing mine."

CHAPTER 16
Deplorable

After the nurse delivered my meds, I lay in bed that night and thought about Anna. She was the most impressive college student I'd ever met, and maybe one of the most amazing people I'd ever know.

The courage and strength it must take to deal with the loss of three family members and still live a productive, happy life is unthinkable.

I replayed the conversation a dozen times as my eyes grew heavy. The anger I'd felt on Monday when I believed Anna was hiding the truth about her identity echoed in my head, but I also heard myself telling lies, hiding the truth about who I really was. Hypocrisy is the second-worst lie. Omission is the first. I was guilty of both.

It was the medication, and not a clear conscience, that allowed me to sleep, but my sins drove the nightmares. I dreamed Anna had the same reaction as me when she discovered my lie. In my dream, I saw her tearing up the pages I'd written for her and running from the room, lashing out at everyone in sight. I saw her bound and sedated, just as I'd been. Watching her struggling against the leather straps and gritting her teeth in anger left me aching to free her. It sickened me, and in my sleep, I vowed to tell her everything, even if it destroyed all possibility of a relationship between us.

* * *

Gladys's voice yanked me from sleep. "I saw they let your daughter—or whoever she is—come back and see you yesterday. How was that?" She slid my breakfast plate onto the table.

"Yeah," I said, forcing my eyes open. "Dr. Oliver said I'd been good enough to earn a visit."

Gladys laughed. "You've clearly got that doctor-man fooled."

Through an exaggerated yawn, I said, "I think you're right."

"Yeah, I'm right a lot, so get used to it. Now eat your breakfast, sleepyhead. It looks like you've got a big day ahead of you."

I sat up. "What are you talking about?"

She motioned into the hallway with her head. "All them reporter people is out there waitin' to see you."

"You've got to be kidding me."

Gladys shook her head, "No, sir. I'm serious as a case of diarrhea at the arm-wrestling contest."

"Ooh, Gladys, that's disgusting."

She looked over the rim of her glasses. "Yep, it sure is, but you've got to admit it's serious."

"What do they want?"

She scoffed. "How the devil would I know what people like that want? I just bring you a plate of food twice a day. I ain't your secretary."

"Thank you, Gladys." I leaned in. "I like you a lot better than the supper guy."

"Well, of course you do, honey. Now you behave and act like you've got some sense. Don't go throwin' none of them reporter people through the window. You hear me?"

"I'll do my best, Gladys, but I can't make any promises."

She giggled. "Well, if you gonna do it, you yell for Gladys first, cause I sure don't wanna miss watchin' that."

"Now, that's a promise I can make."

"Bye, sugar. Enjoy your breakfast."

The hospital could have used a thousand more people just like Gladys. She was a treasure.

I finished my breakfast and took advantage of the shower. I took more showers that week than I'd taken in the previous year combined, and every one of them felt like heaven.

When I came out of the bathroom, a blonde woman with too much lipstick and far too much energy leapt from the ugly brown chair.

"Hey, Mr. Millhouse. I'm Denise Thompson, the public relations officer for the hospital. It's so good to finally meet you."

She practically galloped across the room with her hand outstretched. I shook it warily and almost pinched myself to be sure I wasn't imagining her.

"So, we've got a treat for you this morning, and you're going to love it. There's a reporter from the Knoxville News Sentinel, one from USA Today, and a camera crew from WATE-TV6. What shirts do you have?" She sounded like an auctioneer on cocaine.

"I don't have any shirts. Well, I have a T-shirt from the UT English department, but I don't know where it is."

"That's okay, that's okay. It's not a problem. We can work around that. What size are you?" She spoke faster than I could listen.

I held up my arms and looked down at myself. "I don't know. I'm this size."

Her eyes moved almost as quickly as her lips. "Okay, I've got this. Are you okay to wait here?"

I looked around the familiar room. "This is where I live, so, yeah, I'm okay here."

"Super! Don't talk with anyone until I get you dressed. I'll be right back."

She disappeared like a cartoon character from Saturday morning TV, and I was left standing there in my hospital gown and slippers wondering what was happening.

Denise didn't lie. She did, in fact, return at the speed of sound, and she had two white shirts, a red necktie, and a blue suitcoat.

"No," I said.

She froze in place. "No? What do you mean, no? I need you in a shirt and tie for the interview."

I stood my ground. "No."

"But, Mr. Millhouse, you're going to be on television, and the national news is likely to pick it up."

"I'll wear the shirt, but not the tie and jacket. If that's not good enough, I can do the interview in my gown, or they can go away. Personally, I'd prefer the last option."

"Okay, then, the shirt will have to do. How about pants?"

I shrugged.

She sighed in exasperation. "Don't tell me you don't have any pants."

Another shrug.

"Okay, let me think." She surveyed the room, obviously imagining the camera angles and lighting. "Okay, okay, here's the skinny. We'll put you in your bed wearing your gown, with your blanket draped across your"—she glanced at my bare legs—"lower part."

"Lower part?" I said. "That's what you're going with? Lower part? They're legs, lady. Apparently, you didn't have to take anatomy in public relations school."

She pulled a compact from her bag and moved toward me with a sponge. I raised my hands in front of my face. "What are you doing?"

"I'm going to cover some blemishes and reduce your shine. You look pale."

I backed away from her. "Lady, I'm a homeless dude who got shot in the chest with a shotgun last week. I think the American TV audience would expect me to have some blemishes. Don't you?"

She shook her head as if any ideas other than hers were preposterous. "But the camera is harsh, and we want to put our best foot forward."

"Look, lady. I'm not wearing makeup for you or anyone else. I'll do your interview, and I'll say nice things about your hospital, but you need to calm down."

She huffed. "It's my job to ensure this hospital is represented in the best possible light, and—"

I couldn't let her continue. "Okay, go find someone else to do your interview, and close the door on your way out."

"But, Mr. Millhouse—"

"No buts, lady. You calm down and stop acting like you're the one who belongs up here in the loony bin, or you can go away. It's truly that simple."

The energy visibly drained from her face. "Fine, have it your way, but—"

I held up my hand. "No buts."

She huffed and made her exit.

Part of me hoped she had chosen the go-away option, but that would be too much to hope for. I sat in the bed and raised the head so I could sit at least somewhat upright. To appease Miss Coked-Up Auctioneer Lady, I covered my "lower part" with the white hospital blanket.

When she returned, it would've been easy to believe she was a tour guide. I hoped the reporters found her as absurd as I did.

A thirty-something woman who, based on her appearance, could've been a librarian, broke free of Denise's pack and approached my bed. "Hello, Dr. Millhouse. I'm Kathleen Jeffries with the *Knoxville News Sentinel*. Something tells me you hate this circus as much as I do, so I'm not interested in making it any worse than it has to be. Here's a list of the questions I'd like to ask you. I'll leave it here, and I'll talk with you when things settle down...if that's all right."

Kathleen didn't wait for an answer. She migrated to the back of the pack and disappeared. Her questions were concise, thoughtful, and well-researched. I was impressed.

Denise turned into the ringmaster and began directing the circus. A cameraman placed four lights in a semi-circle and turned my room into a fireball of brilliant white light. I held up my palm, shading my eyes from the oppressive beams.

"Those have to go," I said, trying not to sunburn my retinas.

"The lights are essential for high-def video. There's no other way. You'll adapt in a minute or two. They're absolutely necessary."

"Turn off the lights," I said calmly.

"Mr. Millhouse," began Denise, "you must understand..."

I had reached my limit, but I wasn't going to have another tantrum. The freedom to see Anna meant too much to me. "Turn off the lights," I repeated. "I'd like to see Ms. Jeffries from the newspaper, and no one else."

The lights remained, and Denise began her protest, but I didn't let her get beyond her second syllable. With the curled finger, come-hither signal, I got her to shut up and lean in. Barely above a whisper, I said, "Remind me how to pronounce the word *deplorable*, so when I describe the conditions at this hospital when the camera comes on, I won't sound like an uneducated, homeless bum."

She stood immediately erect and declared, "Okay, okay. Lights out." The cameraman objected instantly, but she shut him down. "The lights go out now!"

Seconds later, the light in the room returned to a suitable brightness to support human existence.

"Thank you, Ms. Thompson. Now, I'd like to see Ms. Jeffries from the *News Sentinel*, please."

Denise leaned close to me. "Mr. Millhouse, we're missing a wonderful opportunity here if you don't do the on-camera interview."

"Listen to me, Ms. Thompson. I'm a crazy, homeless vet who got shot last week. There's nothing I can say or do on camera that will be of any benefit to your hospital. But in addition to all of the negative stuff I am, I'm also a writer, and I used to be a good one. Written words are what I know, so if you'll get these people out of here and leave Ms. Jeffries and me alone, when the *News Sentinel* lands on a million doorsteps tomorrow morning, your hospital will sound like it was carried down from Heaven on the wings of angels, specifically to care for those million readers. If that's the result you want, I'll give it to you. Otherwise, I think I remember how to pronounce *deplorable*."

I admired Denise Thompson's ability to make instant decisions. "Okay, everybody out. Except for you, Kathleen. You stay."

Grumbles and moans answered her order, but the decision had been made. Ms. Jeffries was getting an exclusive.

We talked for slightly less than an hour. I answered all of her provided questions and several more that came up along the way. She was respectful, courteous, and sympathetic—or she was the best actress in the newspaper business.

When she left, Dr. Oliver came in with a smirk plastered on his face.

"What's that look for, doc?"

"I saw what you did, John, and I'm impressed."

I stared up at him. "What are you talking about?"

"You handled Denise Thompson. Nobody handles Denise Thompson, but somehow, you did. What did you say to her?"

I laughed. "Were you watching the whole time?"

"No, not the whole time, but I saw the media circus, and I saw you scatter them to the four winds. So, what did you say to her?"

I raised my eyebrows in mock innocence. "I asked her how to pronounce deplorable."

"You're something else, John." He lifted a leather case from the floor beside my bed. "I have something for you."

"What's that?" I asked.

He opened the flap and pulled out a laptop computer. "I couldn't find the composition book you wanted, but I had this old laptop in my office. It has Microsoft Word installed, but not much else. I figured you could peck out a note or two while you're waiting for that pen and paper I promised."

I took the computer from him and raised the screen. It took several minutes for it to come to life, but when it did, my fingers found the home keys as if I'd never stopped writing. The familiar feel of the keyboard beneath my fingertips brought back emotions and memories I thought had long since abandoned me. The feeling of a story pouring from my brain faster than my fingers could type, and the endless hours of editing, rewriting, and deleting thousands of words that didn't sound how I wanted my readers to hear them warmed a part of me I thought had died.

"Thank you, Dr. Oliver. You didn't have to do this."

He patted my shoulder. "Sure I did, John. You deserve it, especially after that wisecrack about taking anatomy in PR school. That was funny. Now, you've got some writing to do. I seem to remember you promising an up-and-coming novelist you'd write something for her."

I brushed my hand across the keyboard, fanning a layer of dust from the surface. "Aren't we going to have a session today?"

He nodded toward the laptop. "Yes, we are, but the computer is going to play my part. I've got a tee time. I'll see you tomorrow...Cap."

CHAPTER 17
Breakfast Date

By the time the nurse arrived with her tiny paper cup full of pills, I'd put almost ten thousand words on paper...well, onscreen.

"Where did you get a laptop?" asked the pill-bearing nurse.

"Dr. Oliver brought it to me. He thinks writing might be one way to make me less crazy. What do you think?"

She dumped the pills into my hand and held up a cup of water. "How should I know? I'm not the doctor. But it has to be better for you than watching *The Price Is Right*."

"Hey, that's a classic game show. And please remember to spay and neuter your pets."

She took the cup from me. "I think Bob Barker's job is safe if you're his competition. Do you need anything?"

"In fact, I do. I don't know how to save what I've typed. Can you help me with that?"

She actually laughed. "How long has it been since you used a computer?"

I shrugged. "The last time I typed on a computer, it was called a *word processor*."

She pointed toward the disk icon at the upper left of the screen. "Click on that, and then name your document."

Left pinky, right index, right index, left pinky, enter.

"Anna? That's what you want to name your document?"

"Yes, that's it," I said. "I can't think of anything else to call it."

"Okay, then. Anna, it is." She showed me how to navigate to the folder where the document was saved. "That's all there is to it, Mr. Millhouse. I think you've had a pretty good day."

"Yeah, I'd say it's been the best day I've had in a long time."

Sleep came quickly and easily, and the nightmares didn't come at all. I woke to find a copy of the Sunday *Knoxville News Sentinel* folded open to page two, displaying Ms. Jeffries's article: "Former UT Professor and Best-Selling Novelist is Knoxville's Newest Bona Fide Hero." The article was well written, and Ms. Jeffries never misquoted me—not even once.

Anna came dancing through the door with a copy of the paper in her hand, shaking it above her head. "Have you seen this? It's amazing!"

I was barely awake, and she'd been up long enough to read the paper and drive to the hospital to see me. That kid was something else.

"Yeah, I've read it. It kind of makes me sound like a big deal, but the truth rarely shows up in the newspaper."

She slapped my leg with the paper. "You *are* a big deal, professor...I mean, Cap."

"Don't be silly. Have you eaten breakfast?"

"No, not yet. I was kinda hoping we could have breakfast together. How would you feel about a breakfast date with a younger woman? Dr. Oliver gave me permission to take you to the cafeteria...if you want."

"I don't know. You're not really my type." I looked around the room as if there might be someone else I could take on a breakfast date. "But I'd hate to hurt your feelings by saying no, so I guess I'll suffer through it."

"That's sweet of you to make such a sacrifice for me, old man."

I laughed and shoved her off the edge of the bed with my foot. "Let me get cleaned up, and we'll go."

"Oh, I brought you some more clothes. You look pretty funky in those gowns."

"I thought looking funky was cool."

She rolled her eyes. "No, it's definitely not. Hurry up. I'm starving."

I brushed my teeth and showered, but I skipped the shave since Anna was "starving." The clothes she brought fit better than I expected, and when I looked into the mirror, the man who looked back wasn't quite as defeated as he'd been.

We ate the cafeteria breakfast, which turned out to be the same meal Gladys brought to my room every morning, but being among real people who didn't know I was crazy felt nice.

Anna kept rereading the article and quizzing me about every question. "Did you really write your first book because the psychiatrist at the VA told you it would be good for you?"

I swallowed a mouthful of coffee. "I really did, and he was right. It was good for me."

"That is so cool. The first book you wrote was the first novel I ever read that I wasn't forced to read."

"What do you mean? Who forced you to read anything?"

"You know, like in high school. I had to read *Jane Eyre* and *The Scarlet Letter*, but Mom gave me your first book, and that was the first one I ever read because I wanted to."

Hearing her talk about my books as if they were a part of her life was astonishing. I'd never thought of them as anything other than cathartic endeavors for myself that happened to end up selling a few thousand copies. Thinking about my books as having meaning to anyone other than me was a foreign concept, and almost unfathomable.

"Well, it occurs to me that your manuscript is the first and only manuscript I've read in this century."

I could almost see the pages of her mental calendar flipping behind her deep brown eyes. "That's crazy."

I looked around, faking paranoia. "Be careful with that word. Some of my ward mates might be within earshot, and they don't like the word *crazy*."

I caught a grape she threw at me and dropped it into her coffee.

"Hey! That's not funny."

"That's what you get for starting a food fight with a lunatic."

"You're not a lunatic."

"Yeah, I kind of am, though I do think Dr. Oliver's meds are working. But that's not all...."

She perked up. "Oh? What else?"

"I'm not good at meaningful sentiment, but it means a lot that you visit me. I look forward to seeing you, and I've not had much to look forward to for a long time. So, thank you."

"Stop it, silly. You're going to make me cry, and I don't like crying."

I stuck my spoon in her coffee and rescued the grape. It tasted terrible, but I ate it anyway, just to make her laugh.

A young man in blue scrubs strolled by our table. "Hey, Anna. How's your mom?"

She shot a sharp look at me and then immediately toward the man. "Same. No change. But it's still too soon to expect much improvement."

The man grimaced. "That's actually not a bad thing. Stable is exactly what we want to see at this point. Hang in there. It's good to see you."

Anna pressed her lips into a small, thin line. "Yeah, you too. See ya."

"What was that all about?" I asked, almost afraid to hear the answer.

Anna stared at her nearly empty plate. "I didn't want you to know... not yet, at least."

"Know what?"

She bit her bottom lip and sighed, as if telling me was going to be physically painful.

I tried to unburden her. "It's okay. You don't have to tell me. It's none of my business."

She didn't move, and her eyes remained fixed on the remnants of her meal. I suddenly wished we'd stayed in my room for breakfast. Whatever was going on was more than Anna wanted to deal with.

"Seriously, Anna. I didn't mean to pry."

She stood up and focused on the white tile floor. It appeared she was gathering courage for something. As of its own volition, her hand reached for mine. "Come on. Let's go for a walk."

I took her hand and let her lead me from the cafeteria. We walked in silence, but with every step, her confidence and determination seemed to grow little by little. She pulled her hand from mine and slid it inside my elbow, holding my arm.

Without saying a word, we rode the elevator to the fifth floor. The further we walked, the more my mind ran wild, considering the possibilities of what I was on the verge of seeing.

We passed a nurse's station, where a middle-aged woman in cartoon-covered scrubs said, "Hey, Anna. You can't go in right now. You know it's not visiting hours yet."

Ignoring the woman, Anna pulled a pair of paper masks from a box on the corner of the nurse's station and thrust one toward me. "Here, put this on."

She turned to the woman in the absurd scrubs. "We're going in. I doubt she knows, or cares, what time visiting hours are."

Realizing she was fighting a losing battle, the woman offered no argument and returned to her paperwork.

I tied the mask around my neck and above my ears, making sure it covered my nose and mouth as we continued down the corridor. We arrived at a door with a placard reading "Sherry Hollenbeck 527."

Anna pushed her way through the heavy door and pulled me in behind her. Lying motionless in an elevated bed, with a respirator tube in her mouth and every imaginable electrical connection dangling from her body, was Sherry Hollenbeck. Even in her unconscious condition, she was still beautiful in a way so few women are. Hers was a simple beauty; the kind that is exuded from within and doesn't rely on any false pretenses, makeup, or accessories.

Anna reached for her mother's hand and held it tightly against her chest. The rhythm of the heart monitor never fluctuated, and the hiss of the ventilator continued its monotonous task.

"Mom, I know you didn't believe me when I told you before, but it's true. You probably thought I was making it up just to get you to wake up, but I wasn't. He's really here. Mom, this is Professor Cap Millhouse. Professor, this is my mom, Sherry Hollenbeck, and even though it doesn't show on the outside, she's really excited to see you."

I stood in wordless awe of the scene unfolding in front of me. The widow of the man who'd fought and died beside me in the jungles of Colombia nearly twenty years ago was lying lifeless only a few feet away. The woman I'd been too weak to resist when emptiness, loneliness, and the pain of loss consumed us both, and led us to commit the single act that I most regretted in my life, lay broken and suspended before my very eyes.

Anna stepped back and offered her mother's hand to me. "Hold her hand. Tell her you're really here."

Every cell of my body screamed, telling me to turn and walk away, but some force beyond my control and understanding made me reach out and take Sherry Hollenbeck's hand.

The last time I remembered her hand in mine was a day I could never forget, and an abhorrent guilt I could never shed. My knees trembled with every pulse of her heart in the tips of her fingers. I thought the shotgun blast would be the worst pain I could endure, but holding Sherry Hollenbeck's hand with her body clinging to precious life felt as if the weight of the world had fallen on my chest.

"Mrs. Hollenbeck, I'm Captain John Millhouse, and I'm so sorry."

Those were the first words I spoke to her on that day so many years before, and in many ways, another lifetime. I didn't know what else to say, then or now.

"Why would you say that, professor?"

Still holding Sherry's hand, I turned abruptly to face Anna. "What's wrong with her?"

Anna squeezed her eyes closed and bit her lip, gathering the courage to speak. "Mom had a brain tumor, and the doctors removed it the same day you got shot. That's why her head is wrapped in those bandages. She's in a medically induced coma while the swelling goes down and her brain heals. The doctors say there's no way to know how severe the damage is until she wakes up."

I was drowning in Anna's words, and I feared my knees weren't capable of supporting my weight much longer. There were so many questions, but asking them would only cause Anna more pain, and I couldn't do that to her.

She took her mother's hand from mine and laid it carefully by her side. "I love you, Mom. We have to go now, but I'll be back for visiting hours." She kissed her mother's cheek and whispered, "I told you he was really here."

CHAPTER 18
For a Reason

We didn't speak on the way back to the seventh floor. Perhaps neither of us knew what to say or how to say what we were thinking.

After I'd arranged the chairs in my room so we could both look out the window, Anna finally said, "I'm sorry."

I tried to understand what she was apologizing for, but no matter how hard I tried, I couldn't find any part of the past several days for which she would have any reason to be sorry.

I stared at her, unable to avoid seeing Sherry in Anna's young face. "You have nothing to apologize for."

She didn't look at me. "I do. I should've told you my mom was in the hospital here, too. I just thought it was all happening for a reason and you'd think it was weird."

"Weird?" I said. "No, Anna. It's not weird. I can't buy into the theory that everything happens for a reason as part of some grand scheme, but there's nothing weird about your mother coincidently being in the same hospital as me."

She looked up with a frown. "You really don't believe everything happens for a reason?"

"No, I don't believe that a butterfly flapping its wings in Bangladesh can start a hurricane in the Azores. Life is just a random collection of events—chaos, really—that people try to understand by believing it's all part of some great plan."

The look on her face was pity entangled with confusion. "That's sad."

"Sad? Why do you say that?"

"It's sad that you think life is chaos. I think Mom's tumor surgery and your bravery in that bookstore are all part of God's or the Universe's plan to bring you and me together. I think maybe you need somebody who still thinks you're the man you used to be, and I need somebody to believe in my silly dream of becoming a writer."

"Maybe you're right," I admitted, "but wouldn't it be easier for God, or the Universe, or whoever, to just make you believe you're a great writer than to put your mom through the misery of what she's enduring? Do you really think it's fair for whatever power you believe in to let good people like your mom have a brain tumor in the first place?"

She looked away. "I don't know about any of that, but I know you've made this whole thing with my mom a lot easier for me. And you said yourself that meeting me was good for you and that you look forward to seeing me. Do you remember saying that?"

"Yes, I said that, and I'm happy I'm making all of this easier for you, but in the end, I'm still a homeless guy who doesn't have anywhere to go when they kick me out of this hospital. I can't be a part of your life if I'm living on the street."

She looked up at me, a tear trailing down her cheek. "Is that what you want?"

"What do you mean?"

"Do you want to go back to living on the street and not being a part of my life? I mean, I come up here every day, and I get to forget that my mom's lying down there and probably won't ever wake up again. I get to forget about that for a few minutes when I'm with you. And I get to forget that my dad and brother and sister are dead, and that I'm all alone, and it all hurts so much...."

Anna's body convulsed with every gasping breath as pain poured from her soul. I didn't know what to do or say, so I did the only thing that seemed to make any sense in a world where nothing made sense. I knelt beside her chair, wrapped my arms around her, and let her cry.

I believed Anna was a bastion of strength and stability. I believed she had some mechanism inside her that allowed her to deal with all the terrible things life dumped in her lap, but I was wrong. It wasn't strength; it was stubbornness. She simply suppressed the emotions and memories that tormented her and hid them behind good grades, powerful writing, and feigned optimism. She was just as damaged as me. The only difference was I had long abandoned trying to fight back my demons. I had surrendered to them.

There's no way to know how long I held Anna as she cried, and in truth, it didn't matter. What on Earth could have been more important than letting her cry and proving someone cared, even if that someone was a bum?

As her tears reached their end, in sobbing breaths, she said, "Do you have any children?"

Holding her against my chest and ignoring the pain it caused in my shotgun wounds, I said, "No, I don't. Why?"

She pulled away, wiped at her eyes, and swallowed hard. "I think maybe you'd have been a good dad and your life would've been way different."

"Maybe you're right, but it wasn't in the cards for me."

She tried to smile. "Wasn't in the cards, huh? Do you mean like it wasn't in the grand plan you don't believe in?"

I pulled the box of tissue from the table beside my bed and set it in her lap. "Yeah, something like that."

She blew her nose and dried her eyes. "I'm sorry about that. I didn't mean to have a breakdown."

"You never have to apologize for anything, Anna. It's all right. Not dealing with the things that hurt us is what turns English professors and novelists into bums on the street."

"You're not a bum, professor. You've got to stop saying that about yourself. Being negative isn't going to fix anything."

I didn't want to argue with her, but she needed to understand the truth of what my life had become. "I'm just facing reality, not being negative. I'm getting better, but that's a double-edged sword. The healthier I get, the closer I am to being back out on the street. As long as I'm in here, I get three hot meals a day, I can bathe, see you, and my medicine arrives promptly at eight o'clock every night. When Dr. Oliver decides I'm healthy enough to leave, all of that goes away, and I'll be back on the street. Somebody else is sleeping on my cot at the shelter, and I'll go to the bottom of the waiting list to get another one. I can't get a job because I don't have a home, and I can't have a home because I don't have a job. That's the reality of my life."

"That doesn't have to be your reality," she said, setting her eyes on mine.

"What do you mean? I don't have any options. I threw those away a long time ago."

She stared at her fingernails and picked at an imaginary speck on her thumb. "Just hear me out, okay? Don't object or anything until you've heard what I have to say. Can you promise me you'll do that?"

I nodded.

"We've got an apartment..."

I immediately broke my promise and stopped her. "No, Anna, I'm not taking a handout from you and your mom. Besides, she's in a coma, and she'd never approve of you taking in a homeless guy."

"It's not like that," she said, "and you promised to hear me out, so listen. We've got an apartment over our garage behind our house. It's a tiny one-bedroom efficiency, and it's where we keep stuff we're never going to use again. You could stay there until you figure out how to get back on your feet."

I shook my head. "No. I'm not a freeloader. I can't do that."

"Yes, you can, and it isn't freeloading. You'll be editing my manuscript and teaching me to write. That's worth a lot of money, and we can trade rent for that. I hate this term, but it's a win-win. You get a place to stay, and I get an editor and writing coach."

"Anna, you don't know me. You don't know who and what I am. You can't just invite me into your home."

"Stop it! It's not my home. It's a crappy little garage apartment that smells funky and has a leaky roof. Even at that, it's better than living on the street."

"I don't know how to be a writing coach, and I'd be a terrible editor."

She grinned. "Now you're just making up excuses. It's settled. You're moving into the apartment, I'm going to get a book deal, and you're going to make sure I do."

In the previous decade, the greatest kindness anyone had shown me was when Linda would sneak me free coffee and give me stale muffins. I didn't know how to accept kindness, so I couldn't form the words. Anna appeared to take my silence as acceptance.

"Thanks for letting me cry," she said, changing the subject.

"Thanks for letting me let you cry," I said.

"It's time for visiting hours, so I have to go see my mom. Do you want to come?"

I did want to come, but I couldn't. Aside from the fact that I'd have no idea what to say or do in that room, there was another reason I wouldn't be going back to room five-twenty-seven.

"It's not that I don't want to come. I can't. It's against the rules. Psych patients aren't allowed to go into other patient's rooms without explicit permission from Dr. Oliver."

She whispered, "You never know what crazy people are going to do, right?" Then she winked.

"Actually," I said, "predicting the behavior of crazy people seems pretty easy. It's the ones who claim to be sane that are unpredictable."

She stood, hugged me, and made her exit. I watched her leave and then hoped I could remember how to find my document on the laptop. It was a clumsy effort, but after ten minutes of trying, I finally watched the document I'd named "Anna" come to life on the screen.

I heard Dr. Bernstein coming before I saw him. The way he shuffled his feet made his approach impossible to hide.

"Good afternoon, Mr. Millhouse. How are we feeling?"

I hated the way he used the pronoun *we*.

"The *I* of *we* is feeling good, but I don't know how the *you* of *we* is feeling."

He let out a single, one-second burst of laughter. "That's clever. Now, let's take a look at those wounds."

I removed the shirt Anna had given me, and I sat on the edge of my bed. He probed at each of my wounds with his fingertips and made several sounds that couldn't be mistaken for actual words.

Patting my pillow, he said, "Lie back, and let's get these sutures out." He pressed the nurse call button. "We'll have them out in a second."

"Yes, Mr. Millhouse. What do you need?" came the overworked nurse's forced polite response.

"This is Dr. Bernstein. Bring a suture removal kit, some four-by-fours, and a tube of antibiotic ointment."

After a long silence, the nurse replied, "This is the psych ward, doctor. We don't have any of those things up here."

He sighed and dropped his head. "In that case, bring sterile scissors, forceps, and whatever you have that resembles gauze."

Another long pause. "We don't have any of that up here, doctor."

"Oh, for God's sake, I've found the only floor in the entire hospital where no one practices actual medicine. Excuse me, Mr. Millhouse."

He called someone on the telephone and placed an order for delivery, then he thumbed through my chart. The noises he'd made while examining my gunshot wounds were repeated as he carefully studied each page.

A nurse arrived with a tray of goodies, and my stitches were soon on their way to the bio-hazard bin.

Dr. Bernstein peeled the surgical gloves from his hands and dropped them into the receptacle. "Well, Mr. Millhouse, as far as I'm concerned, you can go home. It'll, of course, be up to Dr. Oliver when you actually get to leave, but I don't see any reason to come back up here. I think you're healing just as expected. Do you have any questions for me?"

"Just one," I said. "There's a woman named Sherry Hollenbeck down on the fifth floor. Do you know how she's doing?"

"I'm sorry, Mr. Millhouse, I don't know who that is. Even if I did, I'm not permitted to discuss other patients' conditions with you. You have a good afternoon, and try not to get caught up in any more armed robberies, okay?"

"Sure, doc. I'll keep that in mind." I smiled, enjoying a moment of contemplation. "But maybe some things happen for a reason."

CHAPTER 19
The Boot

"Good Morning, John. How'd you sleep?"

I never knew whose voice I'd hear first when morning arrived. Often, it was Gladys's, but to my surprise, it was Dr. Oliver's on that particular day.

"I slept well, doc. Thank you. You're here early. What's that about?"

"We need to talk, and I wanted you to hear this from me before you heard any rumors."

I sat up. "That doesn't sound good."

"No, John, in my opinion, it *is* good news, but you may not think so at first."

"Okay, let's have it."

"Apparently, you and Ms. Thompson didn't get off on a very good foot yesterday. As I told you, I found it amusing because I'd never seen anyone handle her before you."

"I didn't mean to hurt her feelings, but she was letting things get out of control. In fact, I think she was *causing* things to get out of control. Somebody had to take command and restore order."

He smiled and nodded knowingly. "Oh, you certainly took control. The problem is that Ms. Thompson and the hospital administrator are"—he made air quotes with his fingers—"good friends, if you know what I mean."

"I'm not sure I'm following. What does any of that have to do with me?"

He cleared his throat and pulled up the ugly brown chair. "Like most things in the world, John, it comes down to money. When you came into the ER, you were unconscious, full of buckshot, and bleeding to death. We have an obligation to provide medical care to everyone who comes into the hospital with a life-threatening condition, regardless of a patient's ability to pay."

Suddenly, it all became crystal clear. "Ah, now I'm tracking. Little Miss PR lady went whining to your boss about the crazy, homeless guy hurting her feelings, and now you're kicking me out since I'm not bleeding to death anymore."

Dr. Oliver crossed his legs. "I don't think you're as crazy as you want people to believe, John."

I shrugged. "It's not that. I've been thrown out of a lot of places in the last several years, so I've developed a sixth sense for when the boot is coming."

"Well, don't worry," he said. "It's not happening today. I'm still your attending physician, and until I say you're no longer a threat to yourself or anyone else, we have a responsibility to continue providing care. The problem is, you're doing so darned well. I don't know if it's the nourishment, the security, the medication, the sleep, or Anna. Maybe your marked improvement is from the combination of it all. Sometimes it's difficult to put a finger on what's working. When you leave here, at least some of those factors, and maybe all of them, are going to vanish. That concerns me. I'm sure you've heard of Maslow's hierarchy of needs."

"Sure I have, but I'm not sure I completely agree with him."

Dr. Oliver placed his finger on the tip of his nose. "Bingo. See? I told you. You're far brighter than you want anyone to believe. I agree with Maslow's basic premise. He says people need food, water, warmth, rest, safety, security, intimate relationships, friends, prestige, and the feeling of accomplishment." He paused and glanced toward the ceiling. "I think

I got them all. Anyway, Maslow believed that as those basic needs were met, motivation declines. That doesn't seem to be true for you. That's part of why psychology isn't an exact science. It's more of an art. Even though you don't fall into Maslow's framework of typical psychology, that doesn't mean there's anything wrong with you."

He had my attention, but I couldn't understand where he was going with the discussion.

"Unlike Maslow, I believe the basic needs are food, shelter, clothing, transportation. In the past few years of your life, you've been deficient in all of those basic needs at one time or another. Wouldn't you agree?"

I was listening intently and waiting for some dramatic realization. "Sure, I've been hungry, cold, homeless, down to one set of clothes, and I've not had a car in years."

"We're getting a little off track here, but what I'm suggesting is now that your basic needs are being met, it appears to me you're *more* motivated to succeed."

I let his words sink in before offering my rebuttal. "I think it's Anna."

He tilted his head in curious interest. "What do you mean?"

I motioned toward the open laptop containing the first collection of written words I'd created in a decade. "I think it's Anna who's motivating me. I've not written anything in over a decade, but since she showed up, I've written almost twenty thousand words on a computer I don't know how to use. I agree you and the hospital are meeting my basic needs, but it's Anna who's providing the motivation for me to do more than merely survive."

"That's interesting, John, but without the fulfillment of the basic needs of food, clothing, and shelter, how do you feel Anna will be able to continue to motivate you?"

"I don't know, doc. I'm not the psychiatrist, you are. But when you kick me out of here, I know I have a place to go, so that covers the shelter part."

His eyes widened. "You have a place to live?"

My smile seemed to amuse him, and he instantly appeared anxious to hear my answer.

"Funny you should ask. I got an offer yesterday from a fledgling novelist to come to work as her editor and writing coach."

He raised his eyebrows. "Is that so?"

"It is," I said. "In fact, this young writer happens to have an apartment over her garage that's currently being used for storage. She offered use of that apartment in return for said services."

Instant concern replaced his curiosity. "That's great, John, but how much does she know about your connection with her family?"

"I've been meaning to talk with you about that. I don't think she knows anything about it. She seems convinced our coincidental meeting was all part of some grand, meant-to-be scheme from God or the Universe or something. I want to tell her I knew her father, but the other thing, with her mother, I can't tell her about that."

He drew in a long, contemplative breath. "It's unethical for me to recommend that any of my patients lie; however, there are times when not sharing everything we know is the best policy. I agree you shouldn't tell her what happened between you and her mother. Speaking of her mother, what do you know about her?"

I could see the hesitation in his eyes. He was clearly weighing his obligation to keep patient information private against making sure I knew Sherry Hollenbeck was in a coma two floors below.

I set his mind at ease. "I know she's is in a medically induced coma after surgery to remove a brain tumor."

His relief was evident. "Did Anna tell you that?"

"Actually," I said, "she took me to see her yesterday morning after we had breakfast in the cafeteria. Thank you for okaying that by the way. It was nice to get out of this room."

He took on that confused puppy look. "What are you talking about, John? I didn't okay anything like that."

Realizing Anna's deception, I had to laugh. "Anna must've meant another Dr. Oliver approved the field trip."

"Yes, I'm sure that's what happened," he said. "So, you went into Mrs. Hollenbeck's room yesterday with Anna. Is that what you're telling me?"

"Yes."

"And you saw Mrs. Hollenbeck?"

"Yes."

"And how did that make you feel?"

I nodded. "Ah, so now we've moved from kicking me out of the hospital to a how-did-that-make-you-feel session."

He pointed to the embroidery over the pocket of his lab coat. "See that? It says David W. Oliver, M.D., Psychiatrist. That means I get to turn any conversation I want into a how-did-that-make-you-feel session."

I pointed to the imaginary embroidery on my gown. "See that? Well, no, of course you don't. There's nothing there. But it could say John D. Millhouse, Ph.D., Editor/Writing Coach. That means I can make up anything I want about how seeing Sherry Hollenbeck made me feel."

"This would be a good time for the truth," he pointed out.

I laughed. "So, you get to decide when I tell the truth and when I keep it to myself. Is that how it is?"

He shrugged and pointed back to the embroidery.

"Point taken," I said. "Honestly, it scared the hell out of me, and it brought back a flood of regret, disappointment, and anger at myself, but I also felt concerned."

"Concerned?"

"Sure. I'm concerned about Sherry. Her condition sounds and looks pretty serious. I'm also concerned for Anna. She's lost enough. She doesn't need to lose her mother, too."

"Those are all perfectly rational and valid reactions, John. There's nothing abnormal about any of that."

"Does that mean you're ready to declare me no longer a threat to myself or anyone else?"

"I'm afraid it does. But I have one other interesting bit of news you may find intriguing."

It was my turn to raise my eyebrows. "Let's hear it."

He pulled a slip of paper from his coat pocket. "I found Dr. Murphey, your former psychiatrist from the VA. He's in private practice now and semi-retired. He maintains an office in Sevierville and works a couple of days a week. I spoke with him, and he's agreed to continue your treatment pro bono if you're interested. I know the two of you didn't see eye to eye, but he has a good reputation for getting excellent results for patients like you."

"Patients like me? What does that mean?"

"It means your issues aren't all that rare. You have PTSD and insomnia. Those two conditions are common in combat veterans. We've found the right combination of medication to resolve the insomnia. You're sleeping well, aren't you?"

"Very well," I agreed.

"That's an excellent step, but dealing with the PTSD isn't an overnight fix. There's no simple answer to that condition. It requires careful monitoring of medication, support, and psychological counseling. Those things aren't going to happen on the street, John. In order to return you to a productive member of society, it's going to take dedication and discipline on your part."

"So, what are you saying I should do?"

He didn't hesitate. "I think you should tell Anna about being with her father when he died. That may cause her to rescind her offer of the apartment. If it does, that gives me more leverage to keep you here until we can find a safe, comfortable place for you. Second, I think it would be worth a visit to Dr. Murphey to see if he can help. It won't cost you anything other than an hour of your life, and the benefits could be astonishing."

"You think I should tell her today?"

He nodded. "I do. The sooner, the better, but before we get to that, I need to know what you want."

"I don't understand."

He pulled out his little notepad. "Tell me what a productive, successful life would look like for you."

His questions hit me like a truck. "I don't know, doc. I haven't thought about that for a long time. In order to ever be normal, if normal exists, I'd have to find a way to deal with the regret over what I allowed to happen with Anna's mother."

He made a brief note and looked up. "The way you phrased that response is extremely interesting, John. You didn't say *what* happened with Anna's mother, you said what you *allowed* to happen. That's significant. You've taken responsibility, and even blame, for the event. In many ways, and in most cases, that's the first step to dealing with a problem. However, in this case, I believe you may be taking too much responsibility for a single event that can never be undone. There's no penance you can pay to make it go away. Accepting the fact that you had a lapse in judgment and committing yourself to learning from the event is the strongest way to deal with a situation like this. I know it continues to haunt you, but allowing it to be the defining event of your life gives it far too much power."

Not only was it the defining moment of my life, but also the precipice from which I willingly stopped erasing every good deed I'd done and souring every possibility of becoming human again. "Are you saying I should forget about it and move on?"

"No, John, I'm not saying that at all. I'm saying look at what your life became when you let that event consume your thoughts. I'm not suggesting that fame, money, and prestige are the core of a happy life, but you had those things. You were a well-respected professor, a wildly successful novelist, and in a matter of weeks, all of that vanished because of your perception of a single event."

His words were powerful, but he didn't understand how badly I hated myself for what he kept calling one single event. "I can't just forget about it, doc."

"I'm not suggesting you should forget about it. I'm saying you should make conscious efforts to recognize and acknowledge the event as something you'd never do again and something you'd undo if you could. I'm suggesting you can learn to compartmentalize the event and still have a happy, productive, successful life. The brilliance inside you that made you a great professor is still there. The creativity that made you an incredible writer is still there. I'm suggesting that if you give those positive elements of your life the respect and acknowledgment they deserve, the resultant life you lead will help you overcome the grief you feel over what happened twenty years ago...in a moment of weakness."

I didn't understand why he cared so much about getting me off the street and back on the road to a successful life. Perhaps it was his job to do so, but it felt personal. If he cared for all of his patients the way he cared for me, he was a remarkable doctor and a great man.

"You asked what I wanted."

He poised his pen above the paper. "Yes, I did."

"I want to write again."

CHAPTER 20

The Whole Truth...Mostly

I don't know what I expected. The conversation I would have with Anna about her father would produce one of two distinct reactions. The first, and most likely reaction, would be anger. Anna would be angry with her mother for not telling the truth about me when she'd introduced my books into her life. That reaction would mean I'd be homeless...still. The potential benefit of that reaction would be a slightly extended stay in the hospital. The other possibility was harder to imagine.

Anna arrived, as usual, with one strap of her backpack slung across her shoulder and a brilliant smile on her face. "Good morning, professor or Cap or whatever."

"Good morning, Anna. I have something for you."

She tossed her backpack onto the chair—the ugly brown one—and plopped down on the foot of my bed. "You do? I can't wait. What is it?"

I pulled the computer from the table beside my bed and handed it to her.

She looked at the aged relic. "Um, I have a laptop already, but thanks."

I laughed. "No, goofy. It's not the computer. It's what's *on* the computer. You asked me to write something for you. There it is."

"Are you serious? You really did it?"

"Of course I did it. You asked me to, and I can't say no to you."

She opened the laptop and began to read the first words I'd written since walking away from my life so many years before.

For a writer, it's a terrifying moment when someone else reads their work for the first time. The anxiety and anticipation are almost overwhelming. I so badly wanted her to like what I'd written, but for the first time in my life, I didn't want the credit for having written it; I only wanted her to be happy with it. It was the most personal thing I'd ever written to anyone, and it was never meant for a pair of eyes other than Anna's.

As she read, her lips moved as if she were whispering the words to herself. I'd read exactly like that all of my life. No sounds came from her lips, but she formed every word. I watched as she scrolled down the page until a tiny tear left her eye.

Creating emotion is the writer's purpose. Making a reader feel something, anything, is the essence of writing. Maybe Dr. Oliver was right. Maybe the part of me that was once capable of tearing readers' hearts out was still there. Maybe it was still possible for me to be more than a bum with a chest full of shotgun holes.

I expected her to stop at some point and make a comment, but with every page, she seemed to grow more engrossed with the story. It was a love letter of sorts; not romantic love, but appreciation for the kindness she'd shown me over the previous days. It was the only way I had to say thank you, to tell her how dramatically she'd already changed my life.

When she finished, she closed the laptop and squeezed it to her chest. Tears poured from her eyes, and she looked at me as if I were some mythical creature. "This is the most beautiful thing I've ever read...the most beautiful thing anyone has ever done for me. It's beyond perfect."

I was speechless, and all I could do was smile. She held the computer away and stared at it for a long moment before placing it back on the table, then she wrapped her arms around me and cried in my embrace. "Thank you a thousand times, professor. You can't imagine how much this means to me."

"No, Anna, I'm the one who should be thanking you. You're a re-markable young woman, and you've changed my life. I love the friend-ship we're building, but there's something I have to tell you."

She leaned back and wiped her tears. "What is it?"

I poured a cup of water from the Styrofoam pitcher, probably as a stalling tactic. "It's not easy to talk about, but it's important you know. It may even impact your decision to let me stay in your apartment."

The look of concern on her face grew deeper. "It can't be that bad. Just tell me."

I swallowed the water and gathered my courage. "Do you remember last Monday when I had the outburst that kept us apart for a few days?"

"Sure, but what does that have to do with this?"

I suddenly wished Dr. Oliver were in the room for moral support, but I had no choice other than to continue my story. "Anna, I knew your father."

Her expression turned to blank bewilderment. "What?"

"I was the pilot of the helicopter your father was on when we got shot down in Colombia. I met him two weeks before he died. He was the finest man I ever knew. We worked together every day, and not one of those days went by without him telling me how much he loved your mother and your brother and sister. He carried pictures of them every-where he went. We weren't supposed to do that. We weren't supposed to have anything personal with us in case we were captured. The Army didn't want anyone to be able to use anything personal against us during interrogation."

Her expression was frozen between disbelief and a desperate longing to know the truth. "How did he die?"

I picked at a fingernail, unsure how to continue. "Anna, I don't know how much I should tell you. Your father died bravely, fighting like the warrior he was. He wanted nothing more than to come home to his family. I don't think he knew your mother was pregnant with you at the time. He would've told me."

She squeezed my arm. "Tell me how he died, please."

"The mission may still be classified. I have no way of knowing, but if you truly want to know what happened, I owe you the truth."

She stood and closed the door to my room. "I want to know what happened."

Regardless of my desire to escape, I was committed. "We were on a night infiltration mission for the DEA in Colombia. As I told you before, I was the pilot. Your father was a Delta Force operator, one of the Army's most elite units. He was a truly remarkable man."

The color was entirely gone from her face. "I had no idea. I thought he was just a soldier."

"He was more than that. It would be impossible to describe how brave and endlessly courageous he was. When we got hit, there was no way to keep the helicopter in the air. We crashed into the trees and lost several men during the crash. Those of us who survived fought until we had nothing left to throw at the cartel. We were badly outnumbered and outgunned. There was no hope of fighting our way out of the situation."

Anna squeezed the blanket in her hands, and the muscles in her neck strained. "Was he shot?"

"Yes, he was shot several times, but he kept fighting. He kept shooting until we were out of ammunition. He and I were captured and taken prisoner. He fought our captors like an animal, determined to survive and make it home to see his family. Unfortunately, his wounds were too severe, and he died from blood loss shortly after we were captured."

Anna was crying again, but unlike before, the tears weren't joyful. They were tears of loss and sadness. She took my hands in hers and whispered, "Is that what happened to your thumbs?"

I nodded wordlessly.

"Does my mother know?"

That was the question I wasn't prepared to answer. Dr. Oliver had said, "There are times when not sharing everything we know is the best policy."

I felt I owed Anna the truth, but the whole truth could do nothing positive. I was forced to commit the worst of all lies—the lie of omission.

"Yes, she knows. I spoke with her after it happened. I told her as much as I could at the time. She doesn't know the details I've just told you, but she knows I was there and that I knew your father."

"That's why she loved your books and why she wanted me to read them and love them, too. They were one last connection to her husband and to my father."

I swallowed hard. "I think so, Anna."

"Why didn't she tell me?"

I poured another cup of water, suddenly feeling like I'd not had a drink in weeks.

"I don't know why she didn't tell you. Maybe she wasn't sure the guy who wrote the books was really the same John Millhouse. I did write as Cap and not John. It's possible she—"

Anna put her hand on my arm. "No, professor. It's not possible. She knew. It all makes sense now. Everything about it makes sense. It's why she cried all the way home from the book signing in Huntsville. She said she was emotional about seeing the author of the books that meant so much to her, although that wasn't the whole truth. I think you represented the last connection to my father in her mind. She was reliving the pain of losing him. I was a child, and I couldn't understand any of that back then, but it all makes sense now."

"Maybe you're right," I said.

"I'm absolutely right. Can't you see, professor?"

"See what?"

"All of this was meant to be. All of it. You, her, and me all in the same hospital at the same time. Come on. Surely you don't still believe it's all some huge coincidence."

"I don't know, Anna, but like I wrote in my letter to you, regardless of what or who brought you into my life, I could never have been given a greater gift."

PART II

CHAPTER 21
Home Sweet Home

Dr. Oliver was right. Politics prevailed, and the public relations officer, Ms. Denise Thompson, apparently used her strongest bargaining chip to convince the hospital administrator I was bilking the system.

On the morning of Wednesday, March 14, 2012, I was discharged from UT Hospital and sent on my merry way. When I'd arrived at the hospital, I assume by ambulance, I had owned ten things: two shoes, two socks, one pair of pants, one shirt, one pair of underwear, one green Army field jacket, and two muffins.

When I gathered my things to leave the hospital, my net worth had increased dramatically. I now had three complete sets of clothes, two blankets, a laptop computer I still didn't know how to use, and a ninety-day supply of medication, but those weren't the things I considered to be valuable. I also had Anna.

There was some mysterious hospital policy requiring patients to be wheeled to the loading area regardless of their ability to walk. I argued, but lost, and took my seat in the wheelchair wielded by an orderly who seemed slightly less excited to push me as I was about being pushed.

While the orderly and I were waiting for the elevator to arrive on the seventh floor, Gladys came waddling down the hall in an exaggerated effort to run with something swaddled in her arms. The orderly ignored Gladys, who was busy catching her breath, and headed for the impatiently awaiting elevator. I had other plans.

With a quick flick of my wrist, I locked the brake on the chair's right wheel. The abrupt stop sent the chair spinning through ninety degrees to face Gladys, who was still working on returning her breathing to normal.

The orderly crashed into the handles of the chair and cursed. "We've got to go. I don't have time for this."

I looked up over my shoulder at the grouchy young man. "I told you to let me walk, but you wouldn't listen. Now I'm going to say goodbye to Gladys. If you don't have time to wait, I'm sure I can find my way to the door."

He huffed but didn't persist.

"I'm so glad I caught you before you got away," Gladys said. "All that bitchin' and moanin' you did about losing this raggedy old coat, well here it is, you crazy old fool."

I took my field jacket from her hands and held it in front of me. Holes from the shotgun blast riddled the front, and bloodstains covered over half the garment. "How did you find this?"

"Don't go askin' questions you know I ain't gonna answer. Why do you want that ratty ol' thing anyhow?"

"It's the only coat I have, and besides"—I reached into the pocket and pulled out crushed remains—"I had a couple muffins I didn't want to lose."

She thrust a pair of Styrofoam containers at me. "Get outta here, you old fool. Here, I fixed some breakfasts to go for you and that girl."

I took the boxes and stood from the wheelchair.

Gladys and I embraced until she pushed me away. "Don't get none of that crazy on me."

"Thank you for everything, Gladys. You're a wonderful lady, even when you're calling me names."

The electric doors parted like the Red Sea in front of Moses, and Anna stood by the open front door of her Toyota Corolla.

"Thanks for the ride," I said to the orderly.

Anna took my armload of goodies but refused to touch the field jacket. "What *is* that thing?"

"It's the jacket I was wearing the night I came in."

She grimaced and angled her body away from me and the jacket. "It's disgusting."

"It's the only coat I have," I argued.

"Yeah, well, you're not putting that thing in my car. We'll get you another coat. One without bullet holes and bloodstains."

My first dilemma of the real world had arrived. The field jacket represented my only means of staying remotely warm on the frigid East Tennessee winter nights, but if I was going to return to the realm of real life, a bloody, hole-filled jacket was not coming with me. With a great deal of anxiety and hesitation, I tossed the filthy jacket onto the wheelchair and climbed into Anna's front seat. The orderly started cursing again, but I closed the door.

Anna pulled onto Alcoa Highway, the four-lane road leading from downtown Knoxville, toward the small, aluminum-producing city of Alcoa. "How does it feel to be out of there?"

"I'm a little nervous," I admitted. "A lot has changed since that night in the bookstore."

She reached down and took my hand. "I have a feeling a lot more is going to change for both of us in the next few weeks. I think most of it, maybe even all of it, is going to be good."

"I hope you're right." The scenery passed at sixty miles per hour, landmarks flashing by at a pace appreciably quicker than my feet usually carried me. "It's been a long time since I've ridden in a car."

We turned off the highway and pulled into a long driveway beside a ranch-style brick house with a chain-link fence and garage with a second-story apartment. I sat in silence, looking up at the apartment as we parked. It wasn't easy for me to accept the fact that Anna was willing to give me a place to live—a place with heat and a real bed. I'd been homeless so long, it was going to be a long period of adjustment before I could once again fathom the concept of "home."

"Come on. What are you waiting for?" Anna was already halfway up the stairs before I'd taken my first step out of the car.

The apartment was small, but to me, it was the Taj Mahal. There was a kitchenette with a two-burner stove and oven, a refrigerator, and a sink. The living room had a couch and one chair in front of a television on a metal stand.

Anna pointed toward the back of the apartment. "The bedroom and bathroom are back there. It's not much, but I hope you like it."

I was in awe. "Anna, it's amazing. I don't know what to say."

"Oh, stop it," she insisted. "Come on, let me show you." I followed her into the kitchen, where she opened the cupboard and refrigerator. "I put a few groceries in here, but I don't know what you like. We can go to the store later if you want, but this should be enough to get you started."

I could've easily lived for weeks on the provisions she'd stuffed into the cabinets and shelves. "This is too much. You didn't have to...."

"Cut it out, silly. You've got to eat. Anyway, this is the bedroom and bathroom. It's just a shower stall and no tub. I hope that's okay."

I couldn't believe my eyes. I had a home. For the first time in years, I had a real home. It suddenly became overwhelming, and I had to sit on the edge of the bed. My chin trembled, and I covered my face with my hands, attempting to hide the inevitable tears.

"What's wrong? Why are you crying?"

I wiped my face and motioned around the room. "All of this. It's too much. I didn't—"

"Like I told you, it's meant to be. You'll be back on your feet in no time, and you'll be able to afford a nicer place, but you're welcome to stay here as long as you want."

The only words I could put together were "Thank you," but they felt dreadfully inadequate.

"Let's get your stuff out of the car so you can get settled in. I have to go back to the hospital to see Mom."

We carried my things up the stairs.

"You can set your laptop up over there," she said. "The WI-FI password is "be strong 2-0-1-0," all caps. Oh, and the door key is on the counter beside the sink. I'll be back to check on you later. Maybe we can work on my manuscript."

I had no idea what a WI-FI password was, but everything else made sense. I hung my clothes in the closet and discovered Anna had stocked far more than the kitchen cupboard. There were shirts, pants, and even two jackets hanging in the closet. Staring at the new clothes, I sat on the edge of the bed and noticed a small, black package protruding from beneath one of the pillows. I pulled it free and almost couldn't hold back the tears. In my hand lay a bag of plain M&Ms. With every passing minute, I was more amazed and humbled by her kindness. The world could use about a billion more Annas.

* * *

A gentle rain began, and the leak Anna warned me about showed itself in the bathroom. I placed a cooking pot beneath it and waited for the rain to stop. In the garage below the apartment, there were a few tools and the typical things one would expect to find.

When the rain ended, I took the tools I thought I'd need and climbed on top of the apartment in search of the leak. It didn't take long to find the problem. The flashing around the plumbing vent had been poorly installed and was, without a doubt, the source of the water.

"What are you doing up there?"

I peered over the edge to see Anna staring up at me from the driveway below. "Oh, hey. I was fixing the leak."

"Have you lost your mind? You're going to fall and kill yourself."

I climbed down and put the tools back where I found them. "I hope you don't mind me going inside the garage."

She held the door for me. "Of course not. Did you get it fixed?"

I wiped my hands on a rag lying on the workbench. "I think so. We'll know next time it rains."

She kicked at a pile of debris by the door. "Hey, I'm sorry about that losing your mind comment when you were on the roof. I didn't mean..."

I tossed the rag at her. "Relax. You worry too much. I have some issues, but being overly sensitive isn't one of them. I'm smart enough to know when people are being playful and when they're being intentionally hurtful. I doubt you're capable of the latter."

She threw the rag back at me. "Guess what!"

"I don't know. Tell me."

She beamed with excitement. "Mom moved her hand today."

"That's great. Does that mean she'll wake up soon?"

"Let's go inside and talk," she said. "It's cold down here."

We climbed the stairs to the apartment, and I did the first normal thing I'd done in years. I walked into the kitchen and said, "I can make coffee if you like."

It appeared as if she wanted to say no, but then realized how much I wanted to play host. "Coffee would be great."

As it turns out, coffee making is a perishable skill. I fumbled with the pot, the filter, and even the water. Small victories are important, especially when rebuilding a life, and a successful pot of coffee qualified as my first of what I hoped would be a long string of small victories.

Handing Anna a cup of coffee, I settled into the living room chair that was much nicer than the hospital's version. "So, back to your mom. Does the doctor think she'll wake up soon?"

"They said it's a good sign but that I shouldn't get my hopes up. They've taken her off the drugs that were keeping her in a coma. Now it's just a waiting game. I know they have to be careful about letting families get too excited, but I'm so glad I was there when she moved her hand."

Staring into the coffee cup, Anna said, "This is terrible."

"You're right, but it's the thought that counts," I said, gathering the cups and laughing as she followed me into the kitchen. "I'll keep practicing."

"I think you're going to need a lot of practice. Let me help you." She placed another filter in the coffee maker and poured in two scoops of coffee grounds.

"When are you going back to the hospital?"

She checked her watch. "Visiting hours start at three. Do you want to come?"

There may have been nothing on Earth I wanted more than to see Sherry Hollenbeck come out of her coma, but I had a tremendous fear. "I'd love to, but I don't know if it's a good idea for me to be there when she wakes up. I don't think I'm the face she'll want to see."

"Don't be silly. It would mean the world to her if her favorite author was standing in the room when she woke up."

"I don't know," I said. "Remember the drive home from the book signing?"

Anna's expression fell. "Oh, yeah. I didn't think about that. Maybe you're right. But you will come after she wakes up, won't you?"

"I'd like that," I said.

"Okay, then, it's a date. Do you think we can work on my manu-script when I get back?"

"We can do that," I said. "I've made some notes and done some mark-up. It's a good story, Anna."

She grinned. "I had a good teacher. I learned from you. Reading your books made me believe I could write."

"Your father was a great storyteller. I think maybe it's in your blood."

"Maybe," she said, and kissed me on the cheek before bouncing down the stairs.

I was alone with food in the kitchen, water in the pipes, clothing, warmth from the central heat and air, and a bed on which to rest. That was the base of Maslow's pyramid of human needs. I was safe and secure in a perfect apartment. Intimate relationships and friends are next. I had Anna, and I couldn't imagine having a better friend than her. Prestige and a feeling of accomplishment came next in Maslow's opinion. I'd proven I could patch a leaking roof and relearn to make coffee. Those qualified as accomplishments to me.

I couldn't remember what came next in the pyramid, but at that mo-ment, I didn't care. Life was the best I had known it to be in years, and I had Anna Hollenbeck to thank for making it happen.

CHAPTER 22
That's Not a Real Place

March 16, 2012

Two days later, we'd edited and rewritten the first twenty-five thousand words of Anna's manuscript.

She closed her laptop and stretched her arms above her head. "Aren't you supposed to go back to see the doctor?"

Somewhat embarrassed, I said, "I don't have insurance or money, so I can't go back to UT. There's a psychiatrist in Sevierville named Murphey, who used to be my doctor at the VA. He said he could see me pro bono, but I don't know if I want to go."

"You have to go. I need you."

I wasn't ready for the gravity of that statement. No one had needed me in years. In fact, I wasn't certain anyone ever had.

"You don't need me."

She let out an exasperated sigh. "Yeah, I do. Look at my manuscript. It was terrible, and you've made it beautiful. With mom in the hospital, I didn't have anyone to talk to and hang out with."

"First of all," I began, "your manuscript was far from terrible. First drafts always look like they've been in a train wreck during editing. That's what the editing process is all about. And second, you're in college. You must have dozens of friends to hang out with."

"Thanks. That makes me feel a little better about my manuscript. Were yours that messy?"

Memories of my first novel came flooding back. "I wish you could've seen it. There was more red ink on the pages than black. My editor was amazing, though. She had the heart of a teacher. She'd chop my work into tiny little pieces and set it on fire for ten pages, and then tell me how brilliant I was on the next page. It was the most painful and most exciting part of writing. To look at the manuscript before the edit compared to the finished product was astonishing. The basic storyline was still there, but it's hard to imagine the difference between the two."

"Oh, you're just saying that to make me feel better."

"No, it's true. Every word of it. Writers aren't good editors, and we can never edit our own work. We fall in love with our story and characters. We're emotional and attached. A good editor can look at a manuscript objectively and turn it into a work of art without getting emotionally involved. A good book is a combination of the raw emotion of the writer, coupled with the precision and craftsmanship of the editor. It takes both."

"Does that mean you're not going to get emotionally involved in my manuscript?"

The pained expression on her face made me regret my description of an editor.

"Part of me wishes that were true, but unfortunately, it's too late for that. I'm already invested, and I already love your story. I'll help you clean up the manuscript, but we definitely need to find you a real editor before we try selling your story to anyone."

The broad, innocent smile of a child fell across her face. "Thank you for falling in love with my story."

It was time for me to break her heart again. "I don't think we should thank people for falling in love."

"What? That's ridiculous."

"I don't think we choose to fall in love with people or things. I think it just happens. That's why I don't think hate is the opposite of love."

With her elbow resting on her knee, she propped her chin in her hand. "Oh, so you're a philosopher now, huh?"

That made me smile. "No, nothing like that. I'm just a guy who's made a lot of mistakes in life."

"So," she said, "if hate isn't the opposite of love, what is?"

"I think we have to choose to hate; therefore, a conscious choice can't be the opposite of an emotion like love. I think apathy is probably the opposite of love. To truly not care, to me, that's the anti-love." Maybe I was a philosopher after all. "What do you think?"

She cast her eyes toward the ceiling, considering my question. "I don't know. I've never thought about it like that, but it's an interesting perspective. See? I do need you. You make me think."

I waved a hand through the air. "Thinking is overrated."

"Oh, and your other point about me having dozens of friends at school is BS, too. I'm the youngest student in my class. I can't even drink yet, so I don't exactly spend a lot of time with my classmates."

I crossed my legs and leaned back against the arm of the couch. "Why are you so much younger than everyone else in your class?"

With obvious pride in her voice, she said, "I graduated high school when I was sixteen, so I started college before my seventeenth birthday. I'll graduate this fall, and I won't even be twenty-one yet."

"Are you serious? How did you graduate high school at sixteen?"

She held her head high. "Because I was smarter than everyone in the school...except maybe some of the teachers. But I went to summer school every year and studied my butt off."

"That's amazing, Anna. I don't know how you do it."

She surprised me with an instant answer. "I don't know how everyone *doesn't* do it. Education is important."

"I agree."

She pointed her finger at me. "Nice try, by the way."

"What are you talking about?"

"You tried to change the subject, but I'm smart, remember? You have to go to see Dr. Murphey in Sevierville. I'll drive you."

There was no chance of winning an argument with her, so I surrendered and pulled out the piece of paper Dr. Oliver had given me. She snatched it from my fingertips and immediately began dialing the number. Twenty minutes later, we were on Chapman Highway, headed for Dr. Murphey's office in Sevierville.

The scenery had changed dramatically since the last time I'd left the four-block radius around the Greyhound bus station and mission. As we approached the Sevier County line, I pointed to the northeast. "I grew up not far from here."

"Really?"

"Yes, about ten miles that way, in a place called Mutton Hollow in the Seven Island Community."

She giggled. "Mutton Hollow? You can't be serious. That doesn't even sound like a real place."

It was part of my childhood, so I never considered the absurdity of how it sounded, but I chuckled. "It's real, all right. Although now that I think about it, it does sound funny."

"Yeah, it does. Maybe you could show me where you grew up sometime."

Thoughts of how I'd dismissed my family when they tried to help me quit drinking left me ashamed. "Maybe."

I stared northeast, toward the tiny corner of the Earth where I'd spent the first two decades of my life. It hadn't been a *Leave it to Beaver* situation, but my childhood was far better than most. I should've never become an alcoholic vagrant, but I shunned my family when they tried so hard to keep me from falling off the cliff. Nothing about my condition could be charged to their account; I made the mess, and there was no one to blame other than the man in my shoes.

In downtown Sevierville, a pair of statues adorn the lawn of the county courthouse. A bronze eagle nestled on a rock is a memorial to the veterans of the county who'd given their lives in defense of the country. The second statue is, to the people of the town, equally important. It's a statue of Dolly Parton, also nestled on a rock.

Dr. Murphey's office was on the square downtown.

"Do you want me to come in with you?"

Anna's question pulled me from my daze. I'd been unconsciously avoiding getting out of the car while pretending to look at Dolly.

"I'm nervous," I admitted.

She opened her door and walked around to my side. "Come on. There's nothing to be nervous about. He's your doctor. It's his job to take care of you. I'll go with you so you won't feel alone."

I'd felt alone for longer than I could remember. Somehow, Anna always knew exactly what to say, but even having her by my side didn't quash the dread I felt when I walked through Dr. Murphey's door.

We were greeted by a receptionist wearing an enormous pair of glasses that may have been fashionable in 1974. "You must be John Millhouse."

I nodded, and she stood.

"It's an honor to meet you. I'm Donna. I've been reading about you in the paper. That was really something you did in that bookstore. You're a hero, Mr. Millhouse."

I mumbled, "Thank you, but I just did what anyone would've done."

"Come on back. Dr. Murphey is anxious to see you."

Anna squeezed my hand. "I'll be right here when you come out. There's nothing to be nervous about."

I returned the squeeze. "Thank you. I won't be long."

Dr. Murphey stood and extended his hand. "John Millhouse, as I live and breathe. It's good to see you. Come in, come in. Have a seat."

I shook his hand and searched his face for the man who'd been responsible for my mental health, according to the VA. He had aged almost as much as me, but his voice was still the same.

Donna came back with a pair of coffee cups and set them on Dr. Murphey's desk.

"Thank you, Donna," he said. "Give us about an hour or so."

She nodded and closed the door behind her.

We made small talk over the cups of coffee, and finally got around to the meat and potatoes of the conversation. I told him about Anna and Sherry.

"John, that's a remarkable coincidence for you to wind up in the same hospital at the same time as Sherry Hollenbeck."

"Anna doesn't think it's a coincidence. She thinks it was meant to be."

"Maybe she's right," he said. "Who am I to say differently?"

Was I the only one left on Earth who didn't believe in the meant-to-be theory of chaos?

"So, John, how much does Anna know about your history?"

I swirled the last bit of coffee over the stained bottom of the coffee mug. "She knows I was the pilot the night her father was killed. She knows I've been homeless and screwed up for a while. And she knows I'm her mother's favorite author."

"Yes, indeed," he said. "The books...what wonderful books they are." He pointed to a shelf in the corner of his office. "I have them right up there."

"You read my books?"

"Every word. And they're marvelous."

We discussed the medication Dr. Oliver prescribed, and he approved. "I don't know Dr. Oliver personally, but he's well-respected in the field, and it seems he has you on a combination of medication that's working well."

"He's a good doctor," I said. "He cares about his patients."

"You've been living in the shelter for a while, right?"

I nodded.

"But you have a place now, thanks to Anna."

I continued to nod.

"John, have you forgotten about your VA check?"

I looked up in surprise. "What?"

"Your VA check. You were awarded a medical discharge with disability benefits. What have you been doing with the money from the VA?"

"Other than the money to go back to school, I never got anything from the VA."

He looked confused. "If that's true, you have twenty years of VA disability payments stacked up somewhere. That's your money, John."

I was convinced he had no idea what he was talking about until he punched a number into his phone. He spoke into the handset for several minutes and then put the phone on speaker. "I have Captain Millhouse here, Jeb."

"Hello, Captain Millhouse. I'm Jeb Donaldson with the VA. How are you?"

Unsure what to say, I looked at Dr. Murphey. He motioned toward the phone.

"I'm doing okay," I said. "Thank you, Mr. Donaldson."

"Captain Millhouse, we need an address and bank information so we can send you the money you're owed."

"I don't know my address, but Anna does."

I stood and headed for the door. "Anna, can you come back here for a minute?"

I heard her scamper from the waiting room chair and down the hall. "Is everything okay?"

"Yes, everything's fine. I need to know our address."

She giggled. "I don't know if the apartment actually has an address, but I can give you the house address."

I led her into Dr. Murphey's office. "Anna, this is Dr. Murphey. Doctor, this is Anna Hollenbeck."

He rose and shook her hand. "It's nice to meet you, Anna. I've heard a lot about you."

Anna looked him over. "I've heard a lot about you, too."

"I have Jeb Donaldson on the phone from the VA, and he needs to know John's mailing address."

Anna rattled off the address and gave her phone number as a way to reach me.

"Okay, that's good," came the voice through the phone. "Now I just need some bank information, and we can get your direct deposit started."

"I don't have a bank account," I said, "but maybe I could get one."

"You do that, Captain Millhouse, and when you do, give me a call. Dr. Murphey has my number."

"What was that all about?" asked Anna.

I told her about the VA checks I'd never received, and she programmed Mr. Donaldson's number into her phone.

"We're getting you a bank account today."

CHAPTER 23
Winning the Lottery

As it turns out, bank accounts aren't so easy to open when the applicant has been homeless for over a decade, has no government-issued identification, and has no money.

Anna's spastic, insatiable need to accomplish things as quickly as possible turned out to be exactly what I needed. We acquired a certified copy of my birth certificate from the courthouse, a new social security card, and even a driver's license. I still existed in the databases of the world, but proving my identity required far more than claiming to be Johnathon D. Millhouse.

The Tennessee highway patrolman at the DMV asked, "You're not related to that writer, Cap Millhouse, are you?"

My answer was honest. "I don't think I'm related to anyone famous, ma'am."

She pushed the issue no further and took my picture. With my restored identity in hand, I proudly presented my documents to the assistant manager at the credit union. He would open my new account into which the VA checks would be magically deposited.

The young man typed aggressively on his keyboard for several minutes and then scratched his chin as he read the screen. "Mr. Millhouse, you already have an account with us, but there's been no activity on the account since...this can't be right."

Before he gave me a chance to assure him his computer was most likely correct in its recollection of my last banking activity, the financial wizard had the telephone receiver pressed firmly to his face. For fun, I let him go through the motions with whoever was on the other end, and I winked mischievously at Anna. She giggled and pressed her finger to her lips, encouraging me to be quiet. I learned it takes an assistant manager and a branch manager to comprehend an eleven-year absence from the fiscal world.

"May I see your ID, Mr. Millhouse?" The cheerful young lady whose nametag boasted "branch manager" compared the shiny new license to the information on the screen.

Apparently, her initials constituted the bona fide waving of a magic banking wand, because the assistant manager ceased all questioning of my authenticity upon her blessing.

"Now that that's cleared up, do you want to open an additional account, or start using the existing account again?"

I glanced at Anna, but she offered no guidance. "How much money is in my existing account?"

He wrote down a number on a small square of paper and slid it across the desk to me.

"Six thousand eight hundred dollars?" My hands began shaking, and I dropped the paper back to the desk. "Are you sure?"

"Yes, sir. I'm certain. The last deposit was on June the ninth, two thousand one, in the amount of six thousand one hundred ninety-one dollars. It came from the University of Tennessee office of personnel."

Anna leaned in close to me. "That must have been your last paycheck from the college."

I'd won the lottery. "Can I have some money from that account?"

The assistant manager tried not to laugh. "Well, yes, sir. It's your money. You may withdraw any amount you'd like, but we require a one-hundred-dollar balance to keep the account open."

"In that case, may I have one thousand dollars? And I'd like to have a bank book and some checks. The VA will be making regular electronic deposits into the account soon. Is that all right?"

"Of course. I've changed the address on the account to the address on your driver's license, and you'll receive your checks in the mail within seven to ten working days."

He filled out a withdrawal slip and slid it to me. "If you'll sign at the bottom, I'll get your cash. How do you want it?"

I initially didn't understand his question, but after a moment's thought, I said, "Half in large bills, and the rest in twenties, please."

"I'll be right back, sir."

I whispered to Anna, "Who knew?"

"If you hadn't come to see Dr. Murphey, you would've never known about the VA benefits, and you'd have never come to the bank to open an account. I told you all of this is happening for a reason."

"There you go again with that nonsense."

She put her hand on my knee. "You'll come around sooner or later."

The young man returned with an envelope of cash and an account register. "The teller entered your balance in the register for you. Is there anything else we can do for you today, Mr. Millhouse?"

"I think you've done far more than enough already. Thank you."

As we left the bank, Anna sent a wad of keys flying through the air toward me, and I clumsily caught the metallic blob.

"What am I supposed to do with these?"

"I thought you might want to drive."

"I haven't driven in over ten years. I doubt if I remember how."

"It's just like riding a bike," she said. "You'll do fine."

I hesitantly climbed behind the wheel and started the car. "Do you mind if we go back to Dr. Murphey's office for a minute?"

"We can go anywhere you want. I don't have class today, and I won't be able to see Mom until three thirty, so as long as I make it back to the hospital for visiting hours, everything else is up to you."

I started the car and backed out from the parking spot. Anna was right. It came back to me after a few minutes, and driving felt natural again. Unexcited about the prospect of parallel parking, I was thankful to see two available parking spots in front of Dr. Murphey's office.

"I'll be right back," I said. "This will only take a minute."

I left the car running and pushed through the door into the reception area.

"Mr. Millhouse, we didn't expect to see you back so soon," said the receptionist.

"I just came back to pay for the session."

She looked confused. "There's no charge. Dr. Murphey told me to write it off as pro bono."

"No, I insist on paying. I don't need the charity. I want to pay what's fair."

Still confused, she said, "Hold on just a second. I need to check with Dr. Murphey."

As she stood from her chair, someone came barreling through the front door as if they were being chased by a pack of wolves. To my surprise, it was Anna, standing in the doorway with a look of panic on her face.

"Professor, we have to go! Mom's awake!"

I threw a hundred-dollar bill on the counter and followed Anna back to the car. She took the wheel, and we were soon doing ninety miles per hour on Chapman Highway toward UT Hospital. Surprisingly, no police officers discovered us doubling the speed limit.

We pulled into the same covered loading area where Anna had picked me up, and she slammed the car into park. Before I could react, she was already sprinting toward the hospital, so I parked the car, removed the key from the collection of everything that wasn't a key, and left the tangled, jingling mess on the floorboard.

The walk to room 527 left me questioning everything about the decision I would make when I reached the door. Sherry would undoubtedly be confused, disoriented, and uncomfortable, and my presence could only serve to intensify each of those emotions. I wanted to see her and share in Anna's joy at having her mother fully conscious again, but I didn't have the courage, or perhaps the cruelty, to walk through the door.

In the hallway outside room 527, I sat on the floor with my back to the wall, listening intently to every sound coming from the room. I would recognize Sherry's voice when she spoke, but I feared my reaction. Doctors and nurses came in and out of the room in anxious excitement, but none of them seemed to notice I was there.

I heard a collection of voices I couldn't identify, but none of them sounded like the Sherry I remembered. As I leaned closer to the door, Anna burst into the hallway, first scanning the nurse's station, and finally, my perch.

When her eyes met mine, she clapped in animated excitement. "Come in here! She's awake."

I hesitantly took her hand. "Anna, this isn't a good idea. I don't want to upset your mother. I'd rather wait out here."

"Don't be silly," she scolded. "It wouldn't be right if you didn't come in."

I wasn't sure what she meant, but it was clear she wasn't going to let me off the hook. I scampered to my feet and followed her through the heavy, oversized door and into Sherry's room.

"Seriously, Anna, I don't think this is such a good idea. I really think…"

Anna pulled me toward the bed until Sherry's eyes met mine. I froze. The initial disbelief on her beautiful face slowly morphed into a smile, revealing the single dimple on her left cheek, identical to her daughter's. Her eyes lingered on mine and then swept to Anna's.

"See, Mom? I told you he was here."

Sherry placed her hand over her heart.

"Hello, Mrs. Hollenbeck," I managed to croak.

When I thought it could get no brighter, her smile widened, and she curled her hand into a delicate waving motion.

"It's nice to see you again," I blurted, and immediately regretted my choice of words.

Tears formed in her eyes, and she motioned toward her daughter with an open palm.

"She can't speak for some reason," Anna said. "The doctor isn't sure why, but he says it's too early to know if it's permanent."

The years and trials Sherry had endured left tiny lines around her eyes, but she was as breathtaking as she'd been the day I sat on her couch and detailed her husband's death. It was the day I would commit the most unthinkable and unforgivable act of my life. I didn't want to find her beautiful. I wanted to imagine she had forgotten what I had done. Forgiveness was beyond the realm of possibility, but I silently prayed she could forget.

CHAPTER 24
Believe

The longer I stood at the foot of Sherry Hollenbeck's bed, the more I thought my stomach might explode. The memory and guilt over what I did to that innocent woman years before pounded inside my head like a bass drum. Wishing I could vanish into the air, I quietly crept from the room.

I found myself in a waiting area with a collection of vinyl-covered chairs, tattered magazines, a coffee pot, and a table with a telephone and a lamp. Except for the demons I dragged with me everywhere I went, I was alone.

Recalling how Anna had measured two scoops of coffee in the garage apartment, I fumbled with the pot, not because I wanted coffee, but to give my mind something to do other than drive nails into itself. It didn't work, but my efforts did result in a pot of coffee that resembled watered-down iced tea. It was as bland as my first attempt had been overpowering.

Perhaps in my life there would never be a happy medium. Perhaps I was perpetually spun to the extremes like particles in a centrifuge. I could never find a center, only an outlying limit of existence. If there was a force capable of pulling me back to center, I believed it would be Anna. But the horrible truth I carried could forever repel the joy she might bring, like similar magnetic poles driving against each other by an unseen but overwhelming force.

"Hey, you. Are you okay?" Anna was watching me stare off into space.

"Uh, yeah, I'm all right. I didn't want to be in the way. There's a lot going on in your mom's room, and I felt like I didn't belong."

She crossed the dingy carpet and sat beside me. With my hand in hers, she wore a look of sincerity. "What's going on?"

Dr. Oliver's words rang in my ears.

There are times when not sharing everything we know is the best policy.

"I'm okay, but seeing your mother reminds me of the guilt I'll always carry because of what I did...and didn't do...for your father."

"I get that," she said, "but it's all in the past, and there's nothing you can do to change it. No one blames you for what happened. I certainly don't, and I know my mom doesn't. You have to forgive yourself and live the life God wants you to live. If you don't believe in God, think of it as living the best life you can."

"I believe in God," I whispered. "I'm just not convinced He's in control as much as you give Him credit. If He were, why would He let your father die in the jungle or let your mother lie in that bed unable to talk?"

"Those things are too big for us to understand. We need to have faith that He knows what He's doing, and it'll all work out for the best. That's all we can do. I don't think those are your real questions, though. I think you want to know why God let you go through what you did for the last ten years."

"That's not true. I've never blamed anyone other than myself for anything that's happened in my life, especially not God. I put myself where I am."

She tried to smile. "Maybe everything that's happened to my family and to you has been carefully orchestrated to bring us together. Maybe you're supposed to teach me to write, and I'm supposed to teach you to find the silver linings."

I let myself smile at her, wishing I could share her faith. "You're an incredible young woman, Anna Hollenbeck. I definitely believe you're here to teach me something, but I can't imagine what it is I have to offer you. Go be with your mother. She needs you. I'll be fine here. Besides, I made the second-worst pot of coffee in history. That'll keep me company."

Her sympathetic smile became a brilliant grin. "You and your inability to make coffee. What am I going to do with you?"

"I guess you're going to point to those silver linings when I'm too blind to find them for myself."

"I guess so," she said. "I'm staying here with Mom tonight. You take the car home and get some rest, then come get me in the morning."

"Whatever you say."

I took my nightly medication as prescribed and lay in bed, replaying the incredible events of the day.

I'm not destitute. There's money in a bank account I didn't know I had, and more will come when the payments from the VA begin. I have a home. I have more food than I could eat in a month. And I have Anna.

For the first time in my life, I wanted nothing more.

* * *

Morning coffee was a success. Exactly one-third of my three previous attempts produced a product fit for human consumption. I expected my numbers to improve over the coming days.

Before breakfast, I made a detailed list of every item Anna had stocked in the kitchen. While eating, I pored over apartment rental listings in the morning paper and found several I believed were comparable to my new home.

I didn't know when morning visiting hours were at the hospital, so I guessed nine o'clock. That would give the staff time to recover from serving breakfast before families began piling into the patient's rooms. That also gave me plenty of time to take my list to the grocery store.

The short drive to the hospital was pleasant outside the car, but inside, my mind was racing with anxiety over what might happen when I arrived in Sherry's room.

Until recently, my greatest fears were finding nothing to eat and freezing to death overnight. As terrifying as the reality of hunger and potential hypothermia was, the fear of Sherry Hollenbeck telling Anna I had come to their home just weeks after her father's death left me horrified. Anna would consider my omission a terrible lie, and she would never trust me again. I had tried to tell her several days before, but she assumed I remembered her from the book signing. I let her believe that self-imposed lie, and I was regretting that decision. She deserved the truth, but I could never tell her everything.

My heart pounded as I stepped from the elevator and began the long walk down the hallway toward room 527. I consciously focused on my heart rate and breathing as I reached for the handle. The anxiety caused my temples to throb. The instant before my fingers touched the handle, a young nurse with a tray of test tubes came barreling through the door. I leapt back to avoid being run over, and the woman squealed in surprise. The tray left her hand, and as dozens of test tubes hit the floor, tiny shards of glass and rivulets of blood danced across the tile.

I began apologizing with fervency. "I'm so sorry. I didn't mean to frighten you. I was just reaching for the handle."

The woman grabbed at her heart with one hand and the wall with the other. "You scared the crap out of me. What were you doing there?"

"I was trying to come in. I didn't mean to startle you."

"It's okay, but don't move. There's blood and glass everywhere."

She carefully tiptoed from the crash site and quickly returned with the necessary supplies to clean up the mess.

"Can I help you?" I asked sheepishly. "I feel bad."

"No, I've got it, but I hope I don't have to draw another vial of blood from Mrs. Hollenbeck." She carefully replaced the unbroken tubes in her tray, examining each one as she went. "Nope, we're good. Hers are still intact."

When I finally made it through the door, Anna was laughing hysterically. "What did you do to that poor woman?"

"From the looks of it, I apparently tried to recreate the scene from Stephen King's *Carrie*." My answer did nothing to stop the laughter.

Sherry was sitting with the head of her bed raised and her hands folded in her lap. My eyes fell on her fixed gaze, and her look of amusement transformed into welcoming warmth.

I involuntarily returned the smile, and the anxiety I'd been battling melted into relief. I wondered how a woman who had endured the loss of her husband, two of her three children, and a brain tumor could have the face of an angel.

"Good morning, Mrs. Hollenbeck." I tried to appear as if I weren't staring.

She waved delicately with her right hand, and the look in her deep chocolate eyes said she knew exactly who I was, and that any secrets the two of us held would remain as such.

"I assume you still can't talk."

She slowly shook her head and held up her thumb and index finger in the circular okay sign. She then touched her forehead and let her fingers flair outward as if exploding. I believed she was trying to tell me it was okay that she couldn't talk because she was happy to be awake.

I was almost entranced by her interaction and focus on me, and I wondered if she thought of me as the man pictured on the back of my books, or as the man who came to her door twenty years earlier. I hoped it was the former. The imaginary character of Cap Millhouse, the man whose name was splashed across the covers of my books, was a better person than Captain John Millhouse had ever been, even if he was only a nom de plume.

Anna waved both arms over her head. "Hey, remember me?"

"I'm sorry, Anna. I didn't mean to ignore you. How are you this morning? Did you get any sleep?"

She wrapped her arms around me in a hug I hadn't expected but gladly returned.

"I slept a little, but that chair sucks as a bed."

"Have the doctors said anything about why your mother can't speak?"

She glanced toward Sherry. "Sorry for talking about you like you aren't here, Mom."

Sherry waved a dismissive hand.

"The neurosurgeon came last night and said it's possibly an issue of swelling and could resolve itself in a matter of days. They're doing some scans this morning, and he said he'll know a lot more after that."

"That sounds promising," I said.

Anna nodded enthusiastically. "Oh, yeah. I agree." She paused and glanced at the door. "Would you mind sitting with Mom for a few minutes while I go find some coffee?"

I shot a look toward Sherry, and she nodded in reassurance.

"Of course," I said. "Go. Take your time. We'll be fine."

"Thanks. I just don't want to leave her alone."

She slipped into the hallway with only two backward glances to make sure we were okay.

I moved toward Anna's chair—the one that sucked as a bed—but Sherry lifted her hand, reaching toward me.

I froze in uncertainty. What was I supposed to say or do? Everything about the moment felt wrong. The last time I was alone with her had been the definitive moment of my immorality and despicability. Nothing I could ever do would further remove me from the noble morality every man should demand of himself.

I don't remember consciously taking her hand in mine, but the feeling of warmth and sincerity that flowed through her flesh was unforgettable.

"I'm so sorry," I said.

Her reaction surprised me. She furrowed her brow as if she were confused and began shaking her head in determined movements. Her hand slipped from mine and went to her bedside table, where an ink pen sat on a yellow legal pad.

The legal pad took me back to the VA hospital and Dr. Murphey's office. I quivered at the sight and immediately wanted to disappear.

In a shaky but intentional hand, Sherry wrote something on the pad and offered it to me.

You have no reason to be sorry!

"I would give anything for that to be true, Mrs. Hollenbeck, but I'm sorry for so many things."

She frowned, pointed her finger at me, and reclaimed the pad. When she handed it back, I chuckled.

Don't call me Mrs. Hollenbeck! Sherry!

"Okay, then, Sherry. I'm sorry for so many things. For Payne, for your children, for the brain tumor, and for..."

She placed her hand gently atop mine and slowly shook her head. I was speechless, but I no longer wanted to vanish. She lifted my hand to her lips, gently kissed my knuckles, and motioned toward the door. I looked to see if Anna was returning, but the door was still closed. She squeezed my hand and pulled it tightly beneath her chin, clearly trying to tell me something, though I couldn't piece it together.

"I'm sorry, but I don't know what you're trying to say."

She released my hand and began writing again. I watched the words form on the page beneath her pen.

Thank you for what you're doing for Anna. She adores you.

The words brought a lump to my throat, but I held back the tear that tried to form. "She's amazing, and I'm happy to help. But she's the one who deserves the thanks. She's making me believe again."

Sherry returned another look of confusion.

Believe in what again?

Anna returned before I could respond. Part of me was thankful she did because I didn't have a reasonable answer for Sherry's question. It had been a long time since I'd believed in anything, but out of the blue came Anna, the girl who made me feel something that could only be described as belief.

CHAPTER 25
We Were Brave

A pair of radiology techs arrived and rolled Sherry away for a battery of imaging tests while Anna and I stayed behind.

"Did you bring our manuscript?" she asked.

"*Our* manuscript? It's not ours. It's yours. I can't take credit for any of it."

"We're making it ours, and I like that. Imagine what it would've been like when you wrote your first manuscript if you had a *New York Times* Best-Selling author to help."

"Maybe I would've made the best-seller list in thirteen weeks instead of thirteen months," I joked.

"Whatever. So, did you bring it or not?"

"No, I didn't bring it, but I do want to talk with you about something important."

"What is it?" she asked, obviously a little concerned.

I pulled the list from my pocket. "I went to the grocery store this morning on my way here and added up the prices of everything you put in the apartment for me."

"No! You're not paying for that stuff. It's payment for helping me with *our* manuscript."

"Anna, listen to me. I'll help you for free. I can afford to pay for my own groceries and for the apartment, too. I looked at some listings in the paper, and the apartment is worth at least five hundred a month. I want to pay you. I'm not a charity case anymore. You heard what Dr. Murphey said about the VA sending a check every month. It's important that I pay for what I have."

It was more than a matter of morality. Although I'd never qualify as a psychologist, I thought it was good for my self-confidence to pay for the things I needed instead of relying on handouts. I wanted to believe those terrible days were behind me.

I should've known Anna would find a way to outsmart me.

"Fine," she said. "I'll find an editor and a writing coach and have them give me prices to do what you're doing for me. I'll pay you what they charge, and if it's less than five hundred per month, you can pay the difference in rent."

"You're not going to let me win this one, are you?"

She grinned and shook her head. "Nope. Oh, and I forgot to mention the editor and writing coaches have to be English professors and best-selling novelists. There's no other way to get a comparable price. I'll let you know when I find someone who meets those qualifications. Until then, we'll keep going like it is."

I was amused but not surprised. "You're used to getting your way, aren't you?"

She stared at the ceiling, just like I do when I'm thinking.

"No, not always."

I glared at her.

"Well, most of the time."

I continued my stare. "Okay, pretty much, but what's wrong with that?"

"There's nothing wrong with that," I said. "I think you work hard, study hard, write hard, and deserve to have things your way."

"Thank you. That's sweet of you to say," she offered. "I think I'm going to run home, shower, and change clothes. Do you want to come?"

I looked at the spot where Sherry's bed should be. "I don't know. Maybe I'll stay here so your mom won't have to come back to an empty room. You should grab the manuscript and our notes, though, and we'll work on it this afternoon."

She focused on the ceiling again. "You know, you don't have to go out of your way to be so nice to mom just because she's a big fan. I know it must be weird. I mean, you don't even know her."

I sighed. "That's not at all what I'm doing. In fact, I need to tell you something that's been bothering me. I should've told you a long time ago, but I was afraid."

"Why would you be afraid to tell me anything?"

"I started to tell you in my room upstairs last week, but you gave me a convenient way out, and, like a coward, I took it."

She frowned. "What are you talking about?"

I drew in a deep breath, hoping not only to fill my lungs with air, but also to build my courage. "Remember when I told you I'd met your mother?"

"Sure. You said you met her at the book signing in Huntsville."

"No, I didn't tell you that. You assumed that. The truth is, I met her just after your father was killed. After we were shot down in Colombia, I was the highest-ranking officer still alive, so that meant I was in charge. And that made me responsible for the lives of those men."

She stopped me. "No, professor, you weren't responsible for any of that."

"That's how the Army works. I was the ranking officer, so everything that happened was my responsibility. As part of that responsibility, I felt it was important to personally look in the faces of the family members of the men who died under my command. They deserved to hear what happened directly from me. I went to every wife or mother of every single man who was killed during the operation, and I personally apologized and told them what happened."

Her eyes widened. "You mean you came to my house?"

"Yes, that's exactly what I mean. Of course, you weren't born yet, but I met your mother, and we talked about what happened. After we got shot down, your father looked me in the eye and said, 'If you don't make it, we'll do our best to drag you out of here. If we don't make it, tell our kids we were brave.' I swore to him I would do exactly as he asked. I kept my word to your father. He was brave. He was the bravest man I ever knew, and I wish he could see you now. He'd be bursting with pride."

"You're a good man," she whispered.

I stared into my lap. "I wish that were true, but I've done some unspeakable things that more than undo any good I've ever done."

"I don't think that's how it works," she said. "I think a person is either good inside or he isn't. We all screw up and do things we aren't proud of, but people like you—people who are good inside—are good in spite of the dumb stuff they do. I bet whatever it is you're so ashamed of wasn't half as bad as you tell yourself it is."

I watched her in amazement. "You're quite the philosopher, Professor Hollenbeck."

She grinned. "Not *professor* yet, but I will be...just like you."

"No, you'll never be just like me. You'll always be better. Now, go shower. You smell like a goat. I'll be here when you get back."

She took both of my hands in hers and rubbed her fingers across my battered thumbs. "Just so you know, I'm not upset, and it means a lot that you told me the truth. I'll never be mad at you for telling me the truth."

She continued to amaze me more every day. I knew Sherry must've been an incredible woman and a phenomenal mother to have raised a daughter like Anna.

While I waited for Sherry, I read *Time Magazine* while Saturday morning cartoons played silently on the television hanging in the corner. From the magazine, I learned Vladimir Putin was reelected president of Russia on March 4th, despite allegations of voter fraud. That was the day Ed died in the room with me, and the day Anna cut my hair. I suddenly remembered the day Putin had first been elected president. It was June 12, 1991; the same day I was promoted to captain. Maybe significant days in my life were somehow tied to Vladimir Vladimirovich Putin's political career. I wondered if Anna would have an explanation for that based on her everything-happens-for-a-reason theory.

CHAPTER 26
Busted

I sat alone in Sherry Hollenbeck's room for almost two hours before the technician returned and pushed her bed back into place.

"There, you go," the tech said. "Is there anything you need?"

Sherry shook her head, and he left the room without acknowledging I was there.

I was accustomed to people ignoring me. The homeless become intentionally invisible to most of society, as people make a concerted effort to avoid eye contact for fear of hearing a bum beg for money. Making eye contact with a grungy, unkempt man on the sidewalk forces a person to acknowledge a painful truth about themselves.

That guy must be lazy, an alcoholic, a drug addict, a criminal, dangerous, a deranged wino. If I give him money, he'll just buy liquor or drugs with it, so it's better if I ignore him. Maybe somebody else will help him.

I had been guilty of that same pattern of thought and belief. Most people don't see a dirty, shaggy-bearded man in a tattered field jacket and think, *I wonder if that guy used to be a helicopter pilot, a college professor, or a best-selling novelist.* The stories of how people lost everything they once owned are as varied as the waves caressing the beach. No two are identical, but they all begin swelling someplace offshore, out of sight of human eyes. They build into a powerful wall of water, pushed by an unseen force, until they reach their apex and come crashing down, disintegrating into salty foam as they wash up on the beach. They are ignored and stepped on as society looks out to sea, hoping to see another wave growing and reaching into the sky. It's those high, strong, beautiful waves people want to see, not the washed-up remains of previously beautiful walls of water. Just as the sea doesn't care what humanity thinks of it, the agony and emptiness of years on the street tear away a man's concern for what other's think of him, until he finally believes he truly is invisible and without value.

Sherry Hollenbeck and her daughter, Anna, weren't the kind of women who ignored the foamy, diminished waves that washed the sand from beneath their toes. They were the kind of women who looked down at the shallow, depleted wave as it returned to the depths, and they imagined how it could, once again, grown into a beautiful, powerful crescendo of gleaming water with beams of sunlight dancing through its spray and pelicans gliding across its crown. Sherry and Anna were the kinds of people who believed in what could be, rather than pitying what is.

Some people force smiles when they believe a smile is required, while others refuse to resist smiling when it happens naturally. Sherry smiled with her heart, soul, and every inch of her face when she saw me rising from the chair. Smiles like those can't be forced or faked or bought. They are the epitome of sincerity, and they are impossible to ignore.

I returned her smile as I approached her bed. "How are you feeling?"

Instead of reaching for her legal pad, she nodded and flashed an okay sign. Words aren't always necessary. Some answers—and even some questions—are more powerful without words.

"Good," I said. "You look amazing."

She blushed and covered her face with both hands. When she finally unmasked herself, she was still smiling. With closed eyes, she sheepishly shook her head as if modesty wouldn't allow her to believe my compliment.

"You do look astonishing, Mrs. Hollenbeck. You certainly don't look like someone who just had brain surgery."

She frowned in what could only be taken as anger, and I feared I'd crossed a line. Yanking her pad from the bedside table, she wrote in powerful, deliberate strokes, and then flipped the pad around toward me.

SHERRY!!! NOT Mrs. Hollenbeck!!!

Relieved, I rested my hands on the rail of her bed. "Okay, Sherry, it is."

Her smile returned before her hand went to work scribbling on the pad again. *Anna tells me you're living in our garage apartment and helping with her manuscript.*

"If you're uncomfortable with me staying in the apartment, I can find another place."

She shook her head. *No. I'm glad you're there, and it means so much to Anna.*

"She's an amazing young woman," I said, "and already a brilliant writer. She's very good."

Sherry pointed toward my chest, and I let a questioning look come over my face. *She writes like you.*

I'd never been more flattered. "No, she writes like Anna. You just filled her head with that garbage about me being a good writer, so now she tries to impress you by using my style."

If that's what you think, you don't know Anna at all.

"What do you mean?" I asked.

Anna doesn't try to impress anyone, least of all me. She writes what she writes without caring what anyone thinks.

"In my opinion, that's how writing should be done. It doesn't matter what people think. We don't write for other people. We write for ourselves. If other people enjoy our creation, that's wonderful, but ultimately, writing is about expressing what's inside us, not pleasing someone else."

She cocked her head and stared at me with a look of innocent wonder, then touched her finger to the tip of her nose. *That's how Anna writes...just like you.*

"Maybe," I admitted, "but she's already better than I was at my prime."

How do you know your prime is behind you?

I stared at the words on the page and couldn't believe I would allow myself to consider the possibility of writing again.

She pulled the pad from my hand. *Do you want to talk about what happened?*

Did she mean the afternoon we spent together twenty years ago, or did she mean what happened to make me stop writing? Neither were conversations I wanted to have. The former tore at my soul like a dagger, and the latter was a bottomless pit of embarrassment.

I squeezed the bed rail, and Sherry covered my hand with hers. A worried look on her face asked why I was so sad. I so badly wanted her to understand the depths of my regret over what happened between us all those years before. I needed to apologize in the sincerest way possible, but I didn't know how to start the conversation. I longed for her to hold my heart in her hands and feel the remorse thundering in every beat. If I could only show her how sorry I was, and the lengths to which I would go to undo that moment of weakness, maybe I could be whole again, and maybe I could give her a reprieve from the lingering regret I believed she was harboring from what we'd done.

As I opened my mouth to pour out my soul, she yanked her hand from mine and turned abruptly toward the door.

Anna's voice filled the room. "Well, you two look like you're having a moment. Should I wait outside?"

Feeling like a teenager who'd been caught kissing under the bleachers, I blurted, "No. We were just talking."

Anna giggled. "Neither of you was talking. You were holding hands, and you got busted. I think it's cute."

Sherry wrote, *We were talking about how you write like Cap.*

"Ha! I wish I wrote like him."

I think you do, and he agrees.

Anna dismissed her mother's opinion with a shake of her head. "How did the tests go?"

Don't know yet.

"When will we know?"

When the doctors bring us the results.

Anna seemed to accept that answer and turned to me, "So, do you feel like working on the manuscript?"

I glanced at Sherry as if asking permission, and she shrugged her approval.

Anna and I spent the next several hours correcting grammar and punctuation, and we even rewrote a few passages for clarity and greater depth. After every chapter, Anna delivered her laptop to her mother so she could read what we'd done.

Although she never made a sound, watching Sherry's face told us everything we needed to know about our work. Occasionally, she'd cry. Other times, she'd grin so broadly I thought her face would crack open. There were a few times she frowned and pointed toward the screen. Those were the times that most interested Anna and me. We'd immediately pore over the passage and rewrite it until Sherry loved every word.

The process was entirely new to me. My previous editing experience had been bundling up my manuscript and dropping it off with my editor. Days later, after she'd marked up a few chapters, I'd set about rewriting and correcting the errors she'd found. There was never a third person in the loop. It had always been a repeated process of numerous mark-ups and rewrites until both the editor and I were pleased with the results.

Between Anna's class schedule and Sherry's tests, we continued our triune diligence over the following days. Although Sherry's ability to speak didn't return, she showed dramatic daily improvement and was eventually moved out of intensive care and into a private room.

While Anna was in class, most of my time was spent in the apartment marking up the manuscript, but I took a few minutes every day to write. It didn't take long for the old drug of creativity to readdict me. The pure joy of turning thought into prose had been lost somewhere in the deepest reaches of my past, but feeling that joy return to my life was a freedom I never thought I'd know again.

Every afternoon we converted Sherry's hospital room into an editing studio where the three of us would work together to make Anna's story the best it could be.

* * *

March 23, 2012

Ironically, the day we finished editing, the neurologist declared Sherry well enough to go home. After a bevy of paperwork, Anna, Sherry, and I pulled away from the hospital in Anna's Toyota.

Until that day, I'd never been inside Sherry and Anna's house. It was neat, tidy, and feminine. On the living room bookshelf, hundreds of books, arranged alphabetically by each author's last name, lined the shelves. Halfway through the impressive collection stood six spines I immediately recognized as my five novels, and one English textbook with my name in bold white print. Other than on the shelves of a bookstore an in Dr. Murphey's office, I'd never seen all my books on display in one place. It was simultaneously humbling, flattering, and somehow painful.

"See, I told you my mom was your biggest fan."

Anna was eating a Popsicle and watching me from the kitchen door.

I ran my fingers across the spines. "It's strange to see all of them in one place. It feels like a voyeuristic peek into another lifetime."

Anna tossed the red-stained stick in the trash and wiped her hands on her jeans. "I can't wait to see my books in print. It's going to be so awesome to actually hold my book in my hands and feel it and smell it."

I thought back to the day I opened my first box of books from the publisher. It was like my birthday and Christmas morning all rolled into one. Even though I knew what the box contained, opening it and seeing stacks of my first book was one of the most satisfying experiences of my life.

"There's nothing like it," I said. "Becoming a published author is something less than one-tenth of one percent of people on Earth ever accomplish."

It would've been easy to believe Anna was a three-year-old sitting in utter fascination while listening to a fairy tale. The look on her face was wonder garnished with confidence, and seeing her determination made me proud to have some tiny role in her journey.

"So, now what?" she asked. "How do we get our manuscript published?"

"It's not ours," I reminded her. "It's yours, but I do have an idea."

Her eyes brightened in anticipation.

"It may not work," I said, "but I think it's worth a try. It'll take some research on your part, but I think I know exactly who to call."

CHAPTER 27
It's for You

I would kill for a pizza.

Sherry's note landed in Anna's hand and brought a grin to her face. "That sounds like a great idea. Professor, what do you like on your pizza?"

She waited impatiently for my answer, but it wasn't what she expected.

"I don't remember."

"What do you mean you don't remember? How do you not remember what kind of pizza you like?"

"I can't remember the last time I ate pizza, but I remember loving everything about it."

She laughed. "In that case, I'll take care of everything."

An hour later, a pimple-faced pizza delivery driver rang the doorbell and presented us with two large pizzas covered with every imaginable topping.

Seated around the small kitchen table, we ate from paper plates and wiped our mouths using napkins with tiny pictures of pizza slices strewn about them. I savored every bite and watched Sherry do the same.

She pulled the pen from her pocket and wrote on a napkin. *I dreamed of pizza every day in the hospital.*

Anna wiped her mouth and looked at me. "I've dreamed of being a writer since I was a little girl, and thanks to you, it's finally happening."

Pride beamed on Sherry's face as she watched her daughter, then she scribbled a note and passed it to me. *Thank you for making my daughter's dream possible.*

"I didn't do it," I said. "I just helped with the editing. That's all."

Sherry shook her head, but Anna spoke the words her mother was thinking. "No, that's not all you did. You inspired me to want to write. Your books made me believe I could do it. I would've never started writing if it wasn't for you, and now you're here in the flesh, and it's almost too much to believe. I'm so lucky."

I smiled across the table. "Anna, you're a gifted and talented writer, and that has nothing to do with luck...or me. You're going to be an incredible success. Besides, I'm the lucky one to have met you."

"I told you, professor, it wasn't luck. It was meant to be."

I rolled my eyes. "I still don't know about that, but you walking into my hospital room changed my life in ways you'll never know. I'll never be able to thank you."

"You don't owe me any thanks," she said. "I owe you. It all feels too good to be true, but I'm still waiting to hear your idea about what to do next."

I let another bite remind me how heavenly the taste of pizza is. "I don't know how to find her, or if she's still in the business, but if we can get in touch with my old literary agent, I'm sure she'd love to read your manuscript."

"That would be amazing!" Anna squealed. "And finding her will be so simple. We can find anyone on the internet."

I felt as if I'd been freed from a time capsule. The modern world might as well have been another century. It's hard to believe a decade is enough time to alienate a person from real life.

"Her name is Alisha Rodriguez, and she used to work for a company in Chicago called Peninsula Arts. She represented all five of my novels, and she got a nice chunk of the royalties for doing so."

Anna leapt from the table as if she'd been shot from a cannon, then snatched her laptop from the coffee table and began tapping feverishly on the keys.

Sherry slid another napkin toward me. *Thank you.*

"No," I whispered. "Thank you for letting me be part of this."

"I found her!" Anna came dancing across the floor. When she slid her laptop in front of me, I almost couldn't believe my eyes. On the screen was a picture of my former agent beneath a banner that read "Alisha Rodriguez Agency."

The woman in the picture had aged, but her dark Cuban eyes and confident smile hadn't faded a day. She was still an agent, but she'd obviously left Peninsula Arts and started her own firm. Something about that made me proud.

"Is there a number?"

She clicked on the contact tab at the top of the page, and a list of email addresses and phone numbers filled the screen. Alisha's contact information was at the top, and Anna pulled out her cell phone. Before I knew it, she pressed the phone against my face, and I was listening to the electronic voice on the other end.

"You've reached the office of Alisha Rodriguez. Please leave a message, and someone will return your call promptly. If you are an existing client, please call the private, direct line for your agent."

A long beep sounded, and I spoke into the phone. "Alisha, this is Cap Millhouse. Congratulations on your firm. It looks like you've finally struck out on your own. I know it's been a long time since we've spoken, but I have something I think you should read. Call me at..." I recited the number Anna mouthed to me, and I hung up. "Now I guess we wait."

"It's Friday afternoon," Anna said. "Do you think she might be out for the weekend, or does she check her messages regularly? Do you think she'll call back before Monday? Do you think she'll call back at all?"

Her excitement was contagious. Sherry's grin said she felt it, too, and I was almost as nervous as Anna for the phone to ring.

"I don't know," I admitted. "It's been over ten years since I've spoken with her. She may not even remember me."

Anna scoffed. "How could an agent not remember a five-time *New York Times* Best-Selling client?"

I shrugged. "That was a long time ago. I'm sure she has a whole stable of talent racking up accolades and awards."

Anna found it impossible to sit still. "This is so exciting!"

I felt it was my responsibility to tell her some of the harsh truths about the publishing business. "I know you're excited, Anna, but there are some things you need to know. Getting a publishing deal isn't easy. I submitted over two hundred query letters to agents and publishers after I finished my first manuscript. I got three dozen rejections and nearly two hundred nonresponses that equaled rejections. I had given up. No one thought my manuscript was worth publishing, so I got discouraged and stopped sending out the query letters. I'd settled on teaching English and writing textbooks."

The hope was crumbling in her flushed face. "What changed your mind?"

"Almost a year later, a letter came from Alisha saying she wanted to read my manuscript."

The light returned to Anna's eyes. "What did you do?"

"I pulled it down from a file box in the attic and dusted it off. After a trip to the copy room at the college, I packaged the manuscript and shipped it overnight to Chicago. Then I waited."

"How long?"

Sherry listened as intently as Anna. "I checked the mail every day hoping to see a letter from Peninsula Arts. After forty-four consecutive days of nothing but bills and junk mail, it showed up."

"You had to be over the moon," Anna said.

"Actually, I was so terrified I didn't have the courage to open the letter. It sat on my kitchen table for almost a week, taunting me. I must've picked it up a thousand times but never had the guts to tear it open."

"Are you saying you never opened the letter?"

"Yep, that's what I'm saying. Maybe a couple of weeks after it came, I had a few other professors over for cocktails and discussions about the textbook I was working on. One of them found the letter and asked what it was. I told him, and he wasted no time tearing it open. It held a single sheet of stationery with three well-defined paragraphs. I couldn't read it, but I could see that much through the back of the paper. My heart pounded like thunder in my chest as I watched his eyes read every line."

Anna and Sherry were both leaning toward me with anxious anticipation.

"He tossed the letter across the table and said, 'Congratulations, John. It looks like you've got yourself an agent.' I couldn't believe my ears, but as I read the letter, I learned Alisha thought the manuscript had 'excellent potential for publication' and wanted the opportunity to represent me in efforts to sell it to a major publisher."

"How did that feel?"

"Like my first bite of pizza in ten years.... Unforgettable."

Anna and Sherry grinned at each other.

"I flew to Chicago, signed an agency contract, and waited for Alisha to pitch my story. It took three months, but she was successful, and we sold the first manuscript for more money than I'd make in two years at the university."

"What an incredible story! So, is that what'll happen with our manuscript?"

"Stop calling it ours," I insisted. "And I don't know what'll happen with yours. I'll tell Alisha what I think, and at the very least, I think she'll have one of her agents read it."

Anna covered her mouth. "Oh, my God. I'll never be able to sleep again. This is too much."

Although her excitement was beautiful to watch, it was important for her to understand how slowly the wheels of the publishing world turn. "I know it's exciting, but there's nothing fast about the process. Even if an agent reads it and likes it, nothing happens overnight. In the meantime, I recommend writing a sequel. Nothing sells a first book better than a second book. If it does get picked up for publication, releasing another one on its heels is the best move you can make."

Without a word, Anna wrapped the laptop in her arms and disappeared down the hallway.

Sherry watched her go, then passed me a note. *I guess she's going to start another story.*

I laughed. "I guess so."

She stood and began picking up the paper plates and napkins from our pizza party. I joined the effort by combining the remaining slices into one box and gathering our cups.

"I should get back to the apartment," I said. "Is there anything you need before I go?"

She glanced at the clock on the stove and motioned for me to follow her. We returned to the living room and took a seat on the couch. The arrangement brought back the memory of the day I'd sat beside her on a sofa and detailed her husband's death. I struggled to push the vision of that day to the back of my mind as I watched Sherry thumb through a stack of paperwork from the hospital.

Finally, she pulled out a pamphlet and a typed letter and placed them in my hands. The pamphlet detailed a clinical trial involving stem cell research at the University of Alabama-Birmingham. The study showed remarkable results in the area of cell regrowth in the brains of patients who'd suffered severe brain injuries and surgical trauma. The letter was her acceptance into the clinical trial of the stem cell research project.

Sherry turned the letter over and wrote on the back. *What do you think?*

"I don't know, but it sounds promising. Are you considering it?"

She nodded enthusiastically, but then a somber look overtook her.

"What's wrong?"

She wrote, *It's not your problem.*

I furrowed my brow. "What's not my problem? What is it, Sherry?"

She closed her eyes and sighed before lifting her pen again. *You can't tell Anna. Promise?*

I was growing more confused by the minute. "I can't tell her what?"

With my surgery and the tumor, I haven't been able to work, and it's all so expensive. We have Payne's Army pension, but without me working, it's not enough. I don't know what I'm going to do.

Their home was simple, and they clearly weren't living beyond their means. And Anna had to be on a scholarship.

"Thanks to Anna," I began, "I have a VA check coming every month, and I even got back pay for the years I never collected. I can help."

Again, she took my hand in hers and shook her head.

"Yes," I insisted. "It's the least I can do. You and Anna have changed my life. Without the two of you, I'd still be on the street. I have a home because of you. I have an income because of Anna's insistence on me going back to see Dr. Murphey. It's like Anna keeps saying: maybe all this happened for a reason."

Anna burst into the room with her phone held firmly in her outstretched hand, and again, Sherry jerked her hand from mine.

Anna shot a look at her mother's hand and then back at me. "It's for you, professor. It's Miss Rodriguez."

CHAPTER 28
How Much?

"Hello?"

"Is this really Cap Millhouse?"

"Yes, it really is. Is this Alisha Rodriguez?"

"I've been looking all over for you, Cap! Where the hell have you been?"

I took a long, deep breath. "Well, to tell you the truth, I fell off the Earth for a few years."

"Yeah, I'd say you did, but why?"

I glanced at Sherry and thought about Alisha's question. "It's a long story for another day, but right now, I have a manuscript I think you should read."

She almost screamed. "Have you written another manuscript?"

"No, not me. The author is an English major at UT, and I think she has a lot of potential."

The disappointment in her voice was palpable. "Oh, well, maybe I can have one of my agents read it when they get a lull."

"I really think *you* should read it, Alisha. It's good, and everyone who's read it says it feels like my writing."

"Cap, I'm your agent. Don't BS with me. Did you write it?"

I laughed. "No, but I worked with her on the developmental, line, and copy editing. It's worth a few hours of your time, Alisha."

She cleared her throat. "This is pretty much out of the blue. You disappear for over ten years, and now you're back with some new writer under your wing. I mean, for God's sake, you've not cashed a royalty check in eleven years."

"What?"

"I said, it's all so out of the blue."

"No, no. What did you say about royalty checks?"

"Your books didn't stop selling just because you dropped off the face of the Earth, and now with this whole America's newest hero thing, they're selling like crazy again. That's why I've been trying to find you."

"I'm not following. Are you saying I have uncollected royalties somewhere?"

She laughed. "Yeah, you might say that. They're in my escrow account. Cap, your books are what made it possible for me to start my own firm. You were a rock star back in the day. I can't wait to hear the whole story. It's going to make a great book, I'm sure."

Anna was sitting on the edge of the coffee table, squirming with excitement.

"How much?" I asked.

"How much what?"

"Alisha, focus. How much money is in the escrow account?"

"Oh, that. I don't know, but it's over a million. It's eleven years' worth, and now with the new surge in sales, God only knows what we'll make—especially with the new book you simply must write. I can get you an advance. I can get half a million at least."

I couldn't fathom the dollar amounts pouring out of her mouth. "Slow down. We'll talk about all of that later, but only if you promise to read Anna's manuscript. You. Not one of your agents."

An exasperated sigh came through the phone. "Fine, I'll read it. Email it to me."

I smiled and nodded toward Anna. "Hold on, Alisha. I'm putting Anna Hollenbeck on the phone. She'll tell you about her manuscript, and you can tell her how to email it to you. She'll also give you my bank information so we can get those royalty checks out of your escrow account. Give her your phone number, too, so we'll have a way to contact you directly."

She started into an argument of some sort, but I handed the phone to Anna.

It was fun listening to her tell my agent about the manuscript and making arrangements to get a copy into her hands, but I was more interested in sharing the news with Sherry.

This time, I took her hands in mine, and she looked at Anna as if she didn't feel comfortable with the gesture in front of her daughter. I lifted my hands, offering to keep them to myself, but a look of content resignation came over her face, and she let her hands rest back in mine.

"I have some great news. That's Alisha, my former agent. Well, I thought she was my former agent, but she seems to think she's still representing me. Anyway, she says I have eleven years of unclaimed royalty checks sitting in her escrow account. That's over a million dollars, and she thinks she can get a half-million advance for a new book. I don't have anything to spend that kind of money on, so stop worrying about not working. Everything is going to be fine. I'll make sure of that."

Tears made their way down her cheeks. Even so, she looked angelic behind the pain and relief.

In a trembling hand, she wrote, *John, I can't ask you to take care of us. We're not your responsibility.*

"I wasn't your responsibility, either, but you gave me a place to live and food to eat. More than that, Anna gave me a gift more valuable than anything money can buy. She reminded me how it feels to create a story. She showed me respect and made me believe, for the first time in years, I wasn't a piece of filth beneath society's feet. She gave me back my dignity and humanity. You can't put a price on that."

She leaned toward me and buried her face in my chest. I held her just as I'd done twenty years before in a little house in Muscle Shoals, Alabama. Part of me trembled, and my demons roared. I had to find a way to tell her how that day had tortured me for two decades. I had to find a way to apologize.

Anna cleared her throat. "Every time I see you two, you're practically making out. What's going on?"

"It's not like that," I said. "I was telling her how much it means to me having you two in my life. You've made a greater difference than you'll ever know, and it's time for me to repay some of that kindness."

"Whatever," she said. "I think you've done more for us than we've done for you. Miss Rodriguez says she'll read my manuscript. Oh, and I gave her your bank account information."

"Thank you. There's some royalty money in her escrow account, and apparently, my books are selling again."

She laughed. "I think that's an understatement. I'm going to email her our manuscript so you two can continue whatever *that* is. I mean, how cool would it be if my mom hooked up with Cap Millhouse?"

Sherry was scribbling again. *Did you say over a million dollars?*

I laughed in disbelief. "Yes, that's what Alisha said, but it's hard to believe."

She turned her pad so I could read. *That's your money, John. I can't let you spend it on us.*

I pulled a box of tissues from the coffee table and set it on the couch between us. "What else am I going to do with it? I have everything I need."

She pulled a tissue from the box and wiped at her eyes that told so much. It was obvious she wanted to open up and tell me everything she held inside, but she was trapped in a prison of silence with only slits through which she could pass an occasional note.

"When can you go to Birmingham for the clinical trial?" I asked.

Anna has class every day except Friday, and I can't drive.

"I'll drive you," I said. "I don't have a car, but I can get one."

I have a car, she wrote in hurried script.

"So, when are we leaving?"

Anna returned wearing a triumphant look. "I can't believe I just talked to a real literary agent, and she's going to read our manuscript." She threw her arms around me as if she were eight years old and I'd just bought her a pony.

I returned the hug as Sherry watched with a look of proud satisfaction. She motioned for Anna to sit on the couch between us and then started writing on the pad. She told Anna about the clinical trial at UAB and how I'd offered to drive her there for the treatment.

"How long will you be gone?" she asked. "I can always miss a couple days of class."

Sherry shook her head. *There's no need. It'll only take two days. It's a simple treatment, and then I'll go back every few weeks for observation and more treatment.*

"Can't they do it here?" Anna asked.

No, it's only at UAB.

"When are you going?"

Next week.

* * *

The next morning, Anna pecked on my door as I was having breakfast.

"Come in. You don't have to knock."

Wearing a look of concern, she walked through the doorway and slid into a chair across from me.

"Is everything all right?" I asked.

"I just want to talk about a few things, if that's okay."

"Of course it's okay. You can always talk about anything you want with me."

She drew tiny shapes on the tabletop with her finger. "I don't know. It's probably silly, but what if Miss Rodriguez doesn't like our manuscript? Then what?"

"I'm going to be brutally honest," I said. "Most manuscripts are rejected, so if she doesn't like yours, we'll shop it around to a billion other agents until we find one who does. It's not the end of the world just because one agent tells you to jump off a bridge."

She almost smiled. "Thank you for not blowing smoke up my butt. This whole thing is pretty overwhelming, so it's nice to know you're going to tell me the truth."

"I don't have anything to gain from lying to you."

"Okay, so while you're telling the truth, what's going on with you and Mom?"

Her question terrified me. I didn't know exactly what she was asking, but I didn't like the feeling of guilt that came over me.

Before I could come up with an answer, she said, "I knew the two of you were talking about something yesterday that had her upset. She's been through enough, so it worries me when she gets like that."

A wave of relief came over me, followed closely by the memory of my promise not to tell Anna about their finances.

Anna held up two crumpled pages from the yellow legal pad and slid them across the table.

I read them and sighed. "Your mom made me promise I wouldn't tell you about this."

"Yeah, I know. I read that part, but I'd like to know what you told her. I want to go to grad school next year, but I can get a job instead. I can maybe write for the paper or do some kind of freelance thing. I guess I could even teach high school English or something."

I stopped her. "Listen to me. You're going to grad school. You don't have to get a job. I'm going to take care of everything. You're going to keep writing, and you're going to be the next Nora Roberts."

"But how?" she demanded.

"I think it has something to do with your silly everything-happens-for-a-reason theory."

She cocked her head. "What do you mean?"

"I mean, meeting you has changed everything. You insisted I go see Dr. Murphey. If that hadn't happened, I wouldn't have discovered the VA pension I was supposed to be getting. That alone is enough money for me to help you and your mom while she's recovering, but there's a lot more. Remember yesterday when you gave my bank information to Alisha?"

Listening intently, she nodded.

"Well, it turns out all these years I've been living on the street, my books have still been selling, and nobody could find me to pay me the royalties."

Her eyes widened.

"Those royalty checks have been piling up in Alisha's escrow account, so I'll be receiving a healthy deposit into the account *you* helped me discover I still had at the credit union."

"Professor, that's amazing! I told you it was all meant to be."

I smiled. "Yes, you told me, but there's more. If I write another book, Alisha thinks she can get a big advance from a publisher."

She frowned. "I don't know what that means."

"It's simple," I said. "A publisher writes a check to an author, and it's called an *advance*. That money is then deducted from the royalties when the book starts selling, and the author doesn't get paid until he's paid

226 · CAP DANIELS & MELISSA MASON

back the advance. Depending on what Alisha decides about your manuscript, you may get a small advance."

Her eyes lit up. "Does that mean you're writing another book?"

"I'm thinking about it," I admitted.

"So, are you really going to help us pay the bills until Mom can go back to work?"

"Of course I am. What kind of person would I be if I didn't? You went out of your way to show me kindness I never deserved. As long as I have the means to help, there's no way I could let you and your mother struggle."

"You're an amazing man, professor. This whole thing is too much to comprehend. How can you *not* believe it was meant to be?"

I took my last bite of buttered toast. "It's getting harder and harder for me to argue about that."

"So, about you and Mom. Are you two...."

"No, Anna. There's nothing like that going on."

She locked eyes with me and squinted. "But there could be, right? I mean, you like her, and I know you have to think she's pretty. Everybody thinks she's gorgeous...even the guys at school. I think it's great. That means I'll probably look like her when I get older."

I offered an honest smile. "Your mother is very beautiful, Anna, and you look just like she did the first time I met her. But neither of us is looking for more than a friendship right now."

"But you're not ruling it out in the long term, right?"

I stood and began washing my breakfast dishes. "It's not something I think about."

Anna squeezed in beside me at the tiny sink. "Here, I'll rinse."

I washed and passed the dishes to her as she let the hot water wash away the suds.

"Have you ever been married?" she asked.

"No."

"Why not?"

The honest answer isn't something I'll ever be able to tell her, so I pieced together an answer that wasn't a lie but didn't fully pull back the curtain on John Millhouse, either. "When I left the Army, I went back to school. Then I went to work as an English professor and started writing seriously. There was never time for me to pursue anyone. I would've made a terrible husband anyway since I worked all the time and hardly slept. When things started going downhill for me, I never thought about a relationship. I could barely keep myself alive. What was I going to offer anyone else?"

"I guess that makes sense," she said as she stacked the last dish into the drainer. "But things are different now, right?"

"Yeah, things are different now, so who knows what the future holds. But your mom can do a lot better than a guy like me. Like you said, she's gorgeous. Oh, and she has a pretty amazing daughter, too." I pointed the sink sprayer at her and gave her a quick blast of water.

She giggled. "See? I knew it. You *do* think she's gorgeous. I think she's had a crush on you for a long time. And I think you're a catch, professor. You're a good-looking guy, you're smart, talented, well-educated, and you kind of have a job if you decide to write that book Miss Rodriguez wants. I'm just saying somebody like my mom could do a lot worse than ending up with a guy like you."

CHAPTER 29

Good News Bad News

The drive from Knoxville to Birmingham takes almost exactly four hours, plus time spent in traffic and construction. That hadn't changed since I'd last made the trip some twelve years before.

Sherry, even though she couldn't talk, was a great traveling companion, her taste in music was surprisingly in line with mine. Living on the street doesn't lend itself to keeping up with pop music, so what I remembered was music of the nineties and before.

When Janice Joplin came on singing "Me and Bobby McGee," Sherry snapped her fingers in time with the old song. She pointed toward the radio, then to her lips, and then to my lips.

"No," I protested. "I'm a terrible singer."

She folded her hands beneath her chin as if she were begging.

"Fine, I'll sing, but I warned you, it's going to sound terrible."

When the song was over, she grinned, clapped, and unbuckled her seatbelt. Seconds later, she was on her knees in the seat, leaning toward me, and planting a big kiss on my right cheek.

"You're out of control."

She smiled as if she'd never stop and buckled herself back into the seat. A few pushes of the buttons on the radio and "Jack and Diane" exploded from the speakers. She pointed again at the radio and nodded her encouragement for me to sing. This continued for two hundred miles until I was hoarse. We even did a Jimmy Buffett set that was terrible, but

I laughed, and Sherry grinned as if we were runaway teenagers in her daddy's car.

The Kirklin Clinic of Neurology at UAB is massive but surprisingly efficient. After less than an hour of filling out forms and answering questions, we met Dr. Agnohuri, a neurologist who'd been raised in India but moved to the U.S. to study medicine at the age of sixteen. Her intellect reminded me of Anna's.

Dr. Agnohuri performed a battery of tests and ordered a series of imagery, and I stayed by Sherry's side throughout the ordeal. After a long day of being prodded, scanned, and studied, we found ourselves back in the same exam room we'd met Dr. Agnohuri six hours earlier.

"Okay," she began. "I've looked at your test results, and I have some good news...and some bad news."

Sherry flinched and squeezed my hand.

The doctor pulled up several images on her computer screen. "First, the bad news." Sherry squeezed tighter as the doctor continued. "Look at this image here. It's an extremely complex region of the brain called Broca's area. It turns thoughts into words. It also sends information to another part of your brain called the motor cortex, which is responsible for telling your mouth, tongue, and throat how to form the spoken words. On this scan, we can see these parts of your brain are functioning as they should."

She scrolled through several pages on the screen and pointed to another region. "This part of the brain is called Wernicke's area. It's where the understanding of language and communication occurs. According to the tests we did today, it's obvious this part of your brain is functioning as it should."

Sherry wrote the question I was thinking and handed it to the doctor. *If all the parts of my brain are working as they should, why can't I talk?*

The doctor handed the note back. "That is a very good question. This is the question that led me to look at another part that isn't technically brain matter, but a collection of nerves connecting Broca's area to Wernicke's area. These nerves are collectively called the arcuate fasciculus. Look closely at this image." She pointed toward the screen with the tip of her pen. "Now look at this image of a healthy arcuate fasciculus." She pressed a group of keys, and the image on the screen split into two side-by-side views.

"The image on the left is your brain, and the image on the right is how a healthy arcuate fasciculus looks. As you can see, yours is atrophied."

Sherry wrote, *Why?*

The doctor slid the laptop away and faced Sherry. "You ask all the right questions. The most common reason nerves die is lack of oxygen. I believe something happened during the surgery or the recovery period that left your arcuate fasciculus without proper blood flow. This is why I'm sorry to say you're ineligible for the clinical trial. The stem cell treatment cannot resolve your condition."

Sherry's head dropped, and the doctor reacted quickly.

"That's the bad news, but remember...I told you there was also good news."

The anticipation in Sherry's eyes was sublime.

"There's no way to know exactly what happened to cause this, or precisely when it happened, but I do have a theory." Dr. Agnohuri reached for Sherry's pad. "Let me draw a picture for you."

She sketched for several seconds and then explained her drawing. "This is an oversimplified example of a blood vessel. Blood flows *away* from the heart and lungs, and then back to the heart and lungs, continually delivering oxygen and recovering carbon dioxide. The brain's blood vessels are some of the smallest in the body and are most susceptible to a condition common in commercial divers called decompression sickness. A microscopic bubble of nitrogen becomes trapped inside a vessel, causing the blood flow to stop or diminish. I believe this is what has happened inside the blood vessels serving your arcuate fasciculus. That is the good news."

I asked before Sherry could pull the pad back from the doctor. "How is that the good news?"

She smiled. "That is the good news because we can treat this condition right here in the hospital. If I am correct about the cause of your apraxia—your inability to speak—then we can squeeze that tiny bubble of gas back into solution and restore proper blood flow."

How? Sherry scribbled.

"In a hyperbaric chamber."

Sherry glanced at me and then back at the doctor before writing. *Now?*

"Yes, we can put you in the chamber now."

"Is it dangerous?" I asked, suddenly concerned by the thought of Sherry being inside a recompression chamber and something going wrong.

"That is the best part," said Dr. Agnohuri. "There are almost no risks associated with the treatment. We're going to put you in an oxygen-rich, pressurized environment, in extremely controlled conditions under the supervision of one of the world's most highly respected hyperbaric medicine specialists. Even if the treatment doesn't work, there is no reason to believe it will hurt you."

Sherry quickly wrote. *YES!*

"I will arrange for you to be taken down to the hyperbaric medicine department, and we will soon know if my theory is correct."

Thank you!

"You do not have to thank me. It is what we do, but if I am correct and the hyperbaric treatment resolves the condition, you are welcome."

Within minutes of arriving at the hyperbaric medicine department, Sherry was inside the chamber and on her way to the bottom of the sea.

The hyperbaric medicine specialist, Dr. Raleigh, explained, "We're going to try to crush that bubble of gas Dr. Agnohuri suspects is the culprit. If her theory is correct, we should see some positive results in a few hours."

I sat beside the chamber, peering through the heavy glass at Sherry Hollenbeck. She was lying on her back, covered with a thin, white blanket, the fear on her face laced with cautious optimism. Being inside the tube had to be an unnerving condition, especially for someone who couldn't talk.

An intercom system was built into the chamber for two-way communication, so I held the handset to my face and tried to reassure her. "There's no reason to be nervous. Remember what Dr. Agnohuri said. Even if this doesn't work, it can't hurt you."

She tried to smile, but it was tempered by anxiety.

"Do you want to wait until you come out of the chamber to call Anna?"

She nodded.

The dive—as the doctor called it—lasted two hours and fifteen minutes, but it felt like an eternity from outside the chamber. I could only imagine how it must have felt to be trapped inside. The doctors waited as the final pounds of pressure were slowly bled out of the chamber and Sherry resurfaced.

"If it worked, will she be able to talk as soon as she comes out?" I asked.

Dr. Agnohuri said, "No, not immediately. It will take several hours for the nerves to show any improvement, but we'll see the improvement rather quickly on another scan."

The chamber door opened, and a technician pulled Sherry from the tube. Dr. Raleigh looked into her eyes with a bright light and checked her pulse and blood pressure. "It's normal to feel a little light-headed, so be careful when you stand up."

Sherry stood from the gurney and reached for my hand. I stepped beside her and felt her hand slip into mine. Another squeeze and another smile.

"Do you feel okay?" asked Dr. Raleigh.

Sherry nodded and licked her lips, then put her hand to her mouth and made a drinking motion. A technician put a sports bottle in her hand, and she downed the contents in seconds.

"Okay," said the neurologist, "let's get you into a room and make arrangements for another visit to radiology and an overnight stay."

They placed us in a private room, and a lady delivered dinner on a pair of plastic trays. "I figured you were hungry, too," she said, "so I snuck an extra. But don't tell anybody."

Remembering Gladys, the funny breakfast lady from UT Hospital, I was coming to believe charity among hospital food workers was a common theme.

After dinner, Sherry motioned to her ear and mouth as if making a telephone call.

"Do you want me to call Anna now?"

She nodded.

Sherry's cell phone was in my pocket, but I didn't know how to use it. I handed it to her, and she dialed the number and pressed the speaker button.

Seconds later, Anna answered, "Hello."

"Hey, it's your mom and John. We have you on speaker."

"It's about time you called. I was getting worried. How's it going?"

Sherry gave me a thumbs-up, so I told the story of the diagnosis and hyperbaric treatment.

"Do they think it worked?"

"We don't know yet. They're taking more images later tonight. The neurologist said we should see a difference in the nerves if the treatment worked, but for now, it's a waiting game."

"I wish I could be there with you."

Sherry smiled and nodded.

I said, "I wish you could be here, too."

"Yeah, I know. You'll be home tomorrow, though, right?"

"I don't know, but we'll let you know as soon as they tell us anything."

"Okay. I love you, Mom."

Sherry placed her hand over her heart.

"She loves you, too," I said.

We ended the call just as a radiology technician came in.

"Okay, it's time to take some more pictures of your brain. Would you prefer walking or riding?"

Sherry made walking motions with her index and middle finger, and the technician grinned. "That's what I thought. Follow me."

We wound our way through the halls until arriving at the radiology department. I wasn't allowed inside the lab where the scans were being done, so I parked myself in the family waiting area. An hour later, Sherry emerged, giving me the okay signal.

When the tech emerged from the depths of the lab, he checked for anyone else lurking nearby and whispered, "I'm not supposed to say anything, but your scans look way better than the ones we did this morning."

Sherry hugged me and then briefly hugged the radiology tech.

"Come on, let's get you back up to your room. And don't tell anyone I told you anything."

Sherry made a zipping motion across her lips, and the tech laughed.

Two hours later, a nurse came into the room and checked Sherry's vital signs. "The doctor placed an order for something to help you sleep if you think you're going to need it."

Sherry stuck out her palm, and the nurse poured two pills from a small paper cup. She swallowed the pills and smiled a thank-you to the nurse.

"You're welcome, darlin'. Get some rest. It sounds like tomorrow may be a big day for you."

The nurse turned to me. "I guess you're planning to stay the night, huh?"

"Yes, I am."

"That's fine," she said. "That chair lays down to make a bed, or you're welcome to sleep on the couch. Neither one of those is very comfortable, but they're better than sleeping on the floor. I'll bring you a blanket."

I settled on the couch and soon heard Sherry's breathing become deep and regular. I never went anywhere without my medication, so I took my nightly dose and soon joined Sherry.

CHAPTER 30
Speechless

"John, are you awake?"

I opened my eyes, expecting to see Anna, but she wasn't there. Blinking to clear my vision, I sat up and grinned from ear to ear. "It worked!"

Sherry said, "Yeah, I think it did."

Seconds later, we were wrapped in a powerful embrace neither of us wanted to end. Her body against mine felt familiar, but I refused to let my libido screw up the perfect morning.

I leaned back, holding her at arm's length. "How do you feel?"

"I feel good. It feels amazing to be able to talk again."

We stood, staring at each other, with relief and joy pouring over us.

She placed her hand on my chest and whispered, "Thank you, John."

"Why are you thanking me?"

"I'm thanking you for everything. For what you're doing for Anna, and what you've done for me. I don't know how to say it enough."

"You never have to thank me, Sherry. I just hope this isn't a dream and you really can speak."

She pinched my bicep, and I flinched away.

"Nope, not a dream," she said.

"I guess we should tell someone, don't you?"

She pressed the call button. "I suppose we should."

The nurse spoke through the intercom. "Yes, Mrs. Hollenbeck?"

"I can talk."

"Okay," the nurse said.

Sherry laughed. "Yesterday, I couldn't talk, but today I can."

"Oh! That's you! Oh my gosh, that's great. I'll notify the doctor right away."

The clock on the television showed 7:45 a.m. when Dr. Agnohuri came through the door. "I hear we have some good news this morning."

Sherry sat up. "We sure do. It worked. You were right."

"It's always nice to be right, but it's better to see patients recover. How do you feel?"

"I feel great. I can't tell you how happy I am that we came here. This place is amazing."

The doctor smiled. "I'm also glad you came. Dr. Raleigh will be pleased to hear of another success from his hyperbaric chamber. He likes to call it his magic carpet. If you don't mind, I'd like to do a brief examination and then one more round of imaging. If everything is as I expect, you can be on your way."

"Of course," Sherry said. "Examine all you want."

The doctor shined a light into Sherry's eyes and leaned in closely. She checked her reflexes and strength in her hands. "Everything looks perfectly normal. I'll order the CT and MRI, and I'll see you again before lunch."

I was learning Sherry Hollenbeck was a habitual hugger. Dr. Agnohuri got a hug, the breakfast lady got a hug, and even the radiology tech was a recipient. Perhaps it was part of her personality, but more likely, the hugs were celebratory.

Sherry dialed a number and placed the phone against her ear. "I thought you might like to hear your mother's voice."

From across the room, I could hear Anna screaming in excitement through the phone. After briefly describing what happened, Sherry said, "I'll fill you in when we get home this afternoon. I love you, sweetheart."

Around noon, Dr. Agnohuri showed up with her laptop computer tucked beneath her arm. "Good afternoon. I imagine you're ready to go home."

"That would be nice," Sherry said.

"I think we can make that happen, but I want you to see your scan before you go."

She opened the laptop and placed it on the rolling table. Soon, a pair of images filled the screen. "Here is the first scan of your arcuate fasciculus, and over here is the most recent scan."

Sherry's mouth fell open. "Wow, that's dramatic!"

"Yes, it is. Fortunately, it appears the blood flow was only partially obstructed, so the nerves hadn't completely died. The hyperbaric treatment did exactly what we'd hoped and fully restored the blood flow. As you can see, your nerves responded perfectly and should be back to full health in a matter of weeks."

"I don't know how to thank you, doctor. I never dreamed this could happen so quickly. You're a lifesaver." Sherry rose to offer another hug, and the doctor didn't resist.

"It's patients like you who make my work so rewarding, Mrs. Hollenbeck. I will have the nurse bring in your discharge paperwork, and you may go home."

On the ride back to Knoxville, Sherry and I sang together instead of enduring another one of my pitiful solo performances. The more I heard her talk and sing, the more I loved her voice. It was filled with such sincerity and honesty that every word she spoke sounded like it had fallen from the lips of an angel.

Immediately following Whitney Houston's version of "I Will Always Love You," Sherry's phone rang, and she answered.

"Okay, just a second," she said. She handed the phone to me. "It's Anna, and she's dying to tell you something."

I took the phone from her hand. "Hey, Anna. What's up?"

"Alisha Rodriguez says she wants to represent me. She says she knows she can sell my book in a matter of days. I'm so excited, and it's all your doing. I couldn't have done it without you! Thank you! Thank you! Thank you!"

"That's great news, Anna. I'm thrilled for you, but none of it is my doing. You dreamed it up. You wrote it. You gave it life. I just corrected a few misplaced commas."

"You did so much more than that! Are you on your way home yet? We have so much to celebrate."

"Yes, we'll be home in an hour."

I handed the phone back to Sherry.

"Well," she said, "I'm not sure how I feel about that."

"Feel about what?" I asked.

"My daughter telling you, and not me, that she got a publishing deal. I'm starting to feel a little left out."

I couldn't resist. "What do you expect? You haven't said a word to her in weeks."

"Oh, you're a funny guy, Mr. Writer Boy."

When we pulled into the driveway, Anna came running out of the house. She and her mother hugged and danced around the yard in tears until the neighbors must have thought them to be completely insane.

We finally made it inside to find the small kitchen table set as elegantly as any fine dining establishment in the city.

"What's all this?" Sherry asked.

"I made a celebration dinner. We're celebrating you having your voice back and me getting a literary agent. It's the best day!"

Anna lit candles on the table and served a rack of lamb with roasted potatoes and mint jelly. I couldn't remember the last time I had a meal that good. We ate and talked and laughed for two hours. For the first time—perhaps in my adult life—I felt like I truly belonged at the table.

Sherry wiped the corners of her mouth. "This was the perfect celebration dinner, Anna. Thank you."

I echoed the sentiment.

Anna almost blushed. "I'm so glad you liked it. I don't think I've ever had so much to celebrate in one day. We deserved a great meal today."

Sherry stared into the candle flame, and a somber look came over her face.

The fork in my hand suddenly felt heavy, and I set it down next to my plate. "Is everything all right?"

"Yes, everything is just right, but I'd like the three of us to have a talk."

"Uh-oh," Anna said. "Talks are never good."

Sherry inhaled a deep, calming breath. "No, this one will be good for all of us. I'm sure of it."

We followed Sherry into the living room, where Anna sat in the recliner and Sherry and me on the couch.

"What's this all about, Mom?"

Sherry smiled at her daughter, then stared at the floor for a long moment. "We all have so much to be thankful for. John, you showed up in our lives unexpectedly and made such an enormous impact. My tumor is gone, and I can speak again. Anna may not be so thrilled about me being able to talk, but she'll get over it."

We shared a nervous laugh, and she continued. "Anna, you got a literary agent, and you're on the verge of having your book published. It doesn't matter what we believe about why this happened, but I believe God gave each of us something we wanted and needed."

I couldn't come up with a reasonable argument against her belief.

Anna lifted both hands, palms up. "It's like I've always said, everything happens for a reason."

Sherry nodded. "That's what I want to talk about. Everyone has secrets and regrets we'd give anything to erase. I think it's time to get those out in the open. We're all adults, and the three of us have been brought together for some reason. I believe we owe it to each other to share the things that hurt us the most, and do what we can to overcome them together. After all, who are we to question a force strong enough to make all of this good stuff happen?"

We sat in silence, taking turns staring at each other until Anna finally said, "Okay, I'll go first."

Anticipation beaming from her face, Sherry leaned forward. "I think that's a good idea, Anna. Let's hear it. And remember, no judgment. Whatever we've done or felt or experienced, we're here to support each other and help deal with it, no matter what it is."

Anna curled her legs into the chair beneath her and took a long, deep breath. "Before P.J. and Kristy went off to camp when I was five..."

Sherry gasped and bit at her lip.

"I'm so sorry, Mom. I didn't mean to...."

Sherry shook her head, "No, sweetheart, please go on. That's what this is all about."

"Okay, if you say so, but it's not easy for me." Anna closed her eyes as if searching for courage. "When we dropped off P.J. and Kristy, I was so mad I couldn't go with them." Her voice trembled as she relived the moment. "The last thing I ever said to them was, 'I hate you! Who wants to go to that stupid camp anyway?'" Her body quivered, and her breath came in gasps. "That's the last thing I ever said to my brother and sister before they died. It's like I killed them with my stupid outburst, and I can never take it back. I've prayed every day for them to forgive me, but I know they can't, and I have to live with that."

Sherry began sobbing, and Anna soon lost her battle to fight back the tears. Hearing the agony in Anna's voice and the depth of regret over the words of a five-year-old girl broke my heart.

Sherry wiped her eyes and motioned for Anna to come to her. The two embraced in a powerful hug.

"They've forgiven you, baby. They know you didn't mean what you said. That was a long time ago. I'm so sorry. I had no idea you were carrying this around for all these years. I promise they've long forgiven you."

Anna sniffed and dried her face. "I've never told anyone, and it feels so good to finally say it out loud." Anna's eyes met mine.

"I know I don't have any right to give my opinion," I said, "but I think your mom is right. It was an innocent child's outburst. You didn't mean it, and I'm sure P.J. and Kristy forgave you the instant you said it."

"Thank you," she whispered. "Will you go next?"

The lump in my throat turned into a boulder, and I turned toward Sherry.

She met my gaze. "You need to get it out, John. Trust me. It's okay."

The thought of unleashing my demon into the room terrified me beyond words, but Sherry's reassurance somehow made me believe it might really be okay.

I closed my eyes, relived the moment in my mind, and tried to form the words.

Sherry's hand landed lightly on my thigh. "It's all right, John. It needs to come out."

When I started talking, the words took on a life of their own. I had no control over what came out of my mouth, and it felt as though I were merely an observer.

"It's the thing that sent me spiraling out of control twelve years ago," I began. "I've hated myself for my weakness and immorality since the day I allowed it to happen. The pain, anger, and self-loathing made me stop taking the medication that held the demons at bay for years. When I stopped taking my medication and turned to alcohol, my life imploded around me all because of my regret for that solitary unthinkable act."

Sherry squeezed my thigh. "Tell us what happened."

I closed my eyes and clenched my teeth. "You know what I did, Sherry, and it is unforgivable. I slept with you the day I told you your husband died, and the self-hatred from that day, from that grave departure from all morality, has left me empty, soulless, and tortured for twenty years."

Anna gasped and began to hyperventilate. I couldn't open my eyes. I couldn't face her. If I allowed myself to see her, only hatred would burn in her eyes. She'd never see me as anything other than the horrific monster who took advantage of her mother.

Sherry lifted her hand from my leg and exhaled a labored breath. "John, when my two children died at that camp, part of me died with them. I thought I'd known loss and agony when Payne was killed, but to hear that my children had drowned at a camp where they were supposed to be safe, where they were supposed to be protected, bore a hole in my heart so big I should've never survived it. So much of me didn't want to live through it. So much of me wanted to dive into that black lake with my babies and never come out. Then my beautiful, five-year-old Anna —the result of the worst thing you believe you've ever done—climbed onto my lap and said, 'I still love you, Mommy.' If Anna...your daughter...our daughter...hadn't been there, I could have never survived the grief. My heart would've broken into too many pieces to ever be put back together. So, John, the worst thing you believe you ever did has turned out to be the best part of my life. And our beautiful, brilliant daughter, who is so much like you, is absolutely right. Everything does happen for a reason. Through it all, no matter how badly it hurt, we were brave."

CHAPTER 31
Aftermath

Shock is a word people use when they can't come up with anything else to describe a person's reaction—or absence of a reaction—following a dramatic event. I had no better word than shock for what I was feeling, but Anna's reaction was far different than mine.

"Why!" she kept repeating, her volume and anxiety increasing.

Sherry stared into space. "It was a time in my life when I felt lonely beyond description. When John showed up, he was the last person to see my husband alive. He was—"

Anna threw her feet from beneath her and planted them on the floor. "No, Mom." She pointed at me and yelled, "Why didn't you tell me he was my father?"

"Until I saw the two of you together, I didn't know, Anna."

"Oh, come on, Mom. How could you not know?"

Sherry squeezed her lips together, forming a determined look of confidence and honest resolution. "The timing was uncertain. Payne had been gone less than a month when John came to our house. I couldn't know for sure, so I couldn't tell you with any degree of certainty who your father was. Payne was a good man—an honest and dependable good man. Believing Payne Hollenbeck was your father could never hurt you, but uncertainty and wonder could've caused you to question everything you knew about yourself. I couldn't do that to you."

Anna redirected her gaze toward me. "Did you know?"

I slowly shook my head. "No, Anna. I had no idea. But I saw so much of who I used to be every time I looked at you. In your writing, in your determination, and in so many of your mannerisms."

Anna leapt to her feet. "You're going to ruin everything!" She stormed from the room, leaving me sitting mere feet from the woman who'd changed everything about my life. I watched Anna disappear through the kitchen, and I stood to follow her.

Sherry grabbed my hand. "No, John. Let her go. What do you do when you need time to process something you never expected to learn?"

"I find some quiet place and...."

"Exactly," she said. "That's what Anna does, too."

I let my eyes fall on her tear-stained face, and for the first time in twenty years, I could breathe without the weight of my unbearable sin crushing my chest. "When did you know, Sherry?"

She swallowed hard. "From the day I found out I was pregnant, I suspected it, but without a DNA test, there was no way to know for sure. As I told Anna, what good could come from her knowing I'd been unfaithful to her father only days after his death? I chose to carry that burden until I realized I would've never survived P.J. and Kristy's deaths without Anna. That's when I knew why she was here. She was a gift from God, regardless of who her father was. She was here to keep me alive and give me something to cling to."

"That's what she's doing for me, too, Sherry. A month ago, I didn't care if I lived another day. Most days, in fact, I didn't want to suffer through another freezing night. But since the day Anna walked into my hospital room, all of that changed. It hasn't made any sense until now, but she and I have a connection that can't be explained. She's my helicopter."

The lines that appeared on Sherry's forehead told me I had to tell her the two boats and a helicopter story. It ended with Sherry Hollenbeck wrapped in my arms, both of us crying like children.

As pain gave way to joy, she looked up at me. "Let's go find our daughter."

"Maybe I should go find her alone," I said.

"I think you may be right. She's probably pretty upset with me right now."

"It's a lot for her to process, but she'll soon realize you did everything you thought was best for her."

I walked across the yard and found Anna sitting on the landing at the top of my apartment stairs. She was clutching something to her chest and sobbing softly.

"Is it okay if I join you?"

She didn't look up and only nodded as she bit at her bottom lip—just as her mother did. I recognized the object tucked between her hands as the tattered paperback of my first novel.

I made a million dollars using words to garner emotion within readers, but at that moment, I couldn't come up with any combination to express what I was feeling. I finally stopped trying to curate the words, and I simply let them come. "You saved my life, Anna."

She raised her face and stared blankly at me.

"Until you showed up in my hospital room, my life was over. It had been over for a long time. All hope of anything better had vanished, and I'd given up. You changed all that. You showed up—who knows why—and gave me something to care about. You gave me a reason to want to see tomorrow."

She pawed at her eyes, clumsily wiping away the tears. "Because that's what was meant to be," she whispered.

"Maybe so," I breathed.

She leaned against me, and I wrapped her in my arms. Perhaps the moment lasted only seconds, or perhaps nearly an eternity, but when she spoke again, her words struck me harder than any I'd heard before, or any I'd ever hear again.

"If I could've chosen a man to be my father, it would've been you."

What's a man supposed to say after hearing those words? There's only one response. "I love you, Anna."

As if she were three years old, she said, "Does that mean you're not leaving?"

"Is that what you meant when you told your mom she was going to ruin everything?"

She nodded. "Yes. I was afraid you'd leave, and I wouldn't have you in my life anymore."

"No, Anna. That's not going to happen. I'm not going anywhere."

She hugged me again. "I guess I should go talk to Mom, huh?"

I suppose it was hopeful curiosity that made me creep back into the house minutes after Anna. I stood in the kitchen, afraid to make a sound as I listened to the tearful exchange.

"It's a lot to swallow all at once, Mom, but I'm glad he's the one."

"I know it is, baby, and I'm sorry I kept it from you for so long."

"No, I understand. It's just that I was so afraid he'd leave. That's why I yelled at you. I'm sorry."

As quietly as I'd come in, I slipped back out and climbed the stairs to my apartment.

* * *

In the weeks following the revelation, Alisha Rodriguez sold Anna's manuscript to one of the big five publishing houses, and her first book under the pen name A.E. Millhouse, with a foreword by Cap Millhouse, made the USA Today best-seller list in record time.

On the coattails of the nationwide coverage of the events at the bookstore, my books experienced a commercial resurrection, and Anna and I embarked on a joint book tour, signing thousands of books. Invariably, the line of adoring fans yearning to meet Anna dwarfed the handful of readers waiting to shake my hand. I wouldn't have had it any other way.

Sherry's anxiety over the mortgage and bills quickly became a non-issue. She healed from the surgery, and the initial trauma all of us had felt from the revelation of me being Anna's father healed even faster. Dr. Murphey played a major role in softening the blow such a shock delivered to us. I continued the counseling sessions with him as my doses of medication diminished and I no longer needed the pills to feel human. But the healing hands that restored my sanity belonged to Sherry and Anna Hollenbeck.

The Christian Brotherhood Mission on Central Street received an endowment from what became the Cap Millhouse Foundation. I was able to hire four full-time paid employees to ensure the doors were open twenty-four hours a day so the men and women, like me, who'd once huddled around burning pallets in the alley behind the shelter, could find a safe, warm place to start putting their lives back together. Dr. Murphey and Dr. Oliver volunteered at the mission. It took a long time for most of the people who'd been my homeless family to accept the psychiatric help, but, like me, they came around. Pastor Jonathon, P.J. for short, was a man of remarkable compassion, wisdom, and faith; he replaced the previous fire and brimstone preacher at the mission, and lives were transformed one by one.

The University of Tennessee English department offered me, Professor John Millhouse, a position in their stable of intellectuals, but I declined, accepting instead the role of guest lecturer on creative writing and mental illness in modern fiction.

Anna graduated magna cum laude and went on to become Dr. Anna E. Hollenbeck, Ph.D. Her passion for language and storytelling was second to none. She turned out to be a pretty good barber as well. No one other than Anna would ever again cut my hair.

Sherry, Anna, and I bought the ratty bookstore and coffee shop. We remodeled and stocked the shelves with every imaginable genre. The cashier who'd survived the robbery became our store manager, and we bought a Starbucks franchise and, of course, promptly gave it to Linda. Her first decision as owner of the newest Starbucks in town was to hang a banner above the pastry case that read: "Muffins so good you'll want to shove some in your pockets for later."

About the Authors

Although this is the first time Melissa Mason's name has appeared on the cover of a novel, it is far from her first collaboration with Cap Daniels. Sharing their love of all things nautical, Cap and Melissa owned and operated a sailing charter service on Florida's Emerald Coast for years. They are longtime scuba diving partners, cruisers, copilots, and adventurers. Their common love of education and travel, as well as their appreciation for great food, wine, and people from all over the world, has sent them far and wide, collecting memories, stories, and unforgettable friends. Melissa is a behind-the-scenes creative partner on the Chase Fulton Novels, Cap's best-selling action-adventure-espionage series, and her voracious reader's appetite gives her the "ear" for how fiction should flow, feel, and evoke emotion. Melissa's beautiful style of storytelling is the perfect complement to Cap's gritty character development.

Business ventures, adventure travel, and co-writing is merely the tip of the iceberg of Cap and Melissa's partnership. They're happily married empty nesters who never plan to stop collecting memories together and creating stories from all over the world.

Visit www.CapDaniels.com to join our mailing list to receive our newsletter and release updates.

Connect on Facebook www.Facebook.com/WriterCapDaniels

Made in the USA
Monee, IL
29 April 2020